BEAUTY
and the
BIN

BEAUTY and the BIN

JOANNE O'CONNELL

MACMILLAN CHILDREN'S BOOKS

First published 2021 by Macmillan Children's Books
an imprint of Pan Macmillan
The Smithson, 6 Briset Street, London EC1M 5NR
Associated companies throughout the world
www.panmacmillan.com

ISBN 978-1-5290-3257-4

1 3 5 7 9 8 6 4 2

A CIP catalogue record for this book is available from the British Library.

Printed and bound by CPI Group (UK) Ltd, Croydon CR0 4YY

For John, Ella, and Clara, with love x

CHAPTER ONE

'You have two choices, Laurie. You can either get some food out of the bins to take to the party or you can get back into the car and sulk.'

Laurie got back into the car and sulked.

Unconcerned, her mum picked up the bags. 'Come on, Fern,' she said to Laurie's little sister. 'Last night's rubbish should still be in the containers. We're looking for bagels, salad, strawberries . . .'

'Can I get into the actual bin?' asked Fern, jumping up and down on the spot. Her bracelets, home-made from bottle tops, jangled loudly. 'Like properly inside it? And throw things over to you?'

'But you're the lookout,' said Mum. 'What if the manager comes out and you don't give me the signal in time?'

Laurie pulled her cardigan around her. *Normal people*, she thought, *don't slip around the back of supermarkets and take things out of the bins for free*. She stared out of the window. It was nearly seven o'clock on a Saturday evening and the car park was busy. Shoppers were going through the shiny doors, into the brightly lit aisles to pay for groceries.

Her eyes rested on a girl and her mum – both dressed in this season's statement jeans – who were trying to prise a trolley out of the rack. The mum kept tugging on the handles and then throwing her arms up, panto-style. Laurie couldn't see the girl's face but she was tossing her blonde ponytail.

She's probably laughing, thought Laurie. *Like I'd be, if I hadn't been asked to climb into a bin and splatter myself with yogurt, custard and hummus*. She ran a hand down her jeans. She was wearing her favourite pair – not sausage-tight but not baggy at the knees either.

'Is this about your jeans?' Laurie's mum was back in the car, digging around in the glove compartment. 'I did ask you to wear old clothes, Lau. I mean, look at me.' She was wearing a sweatshirt with the slogan *Less Carbon, More Carbs!* and jeans that were older than Laurie.

'It's not that,' Laurie said quickly. Her mum was clueless when it came to fashion, but she didn't want to hurt her feelings. Anyway, that was the truth. Old clothes were the least of her problems.

Laurie took a deep breath. 'Look at this place,' she said. 'I know it's nearly closing time but you promised it wouldn't be busy, Mum. And it's packed! We could easily get caught.'

Fern's face appeared at the window. 'For what, though? We're not stealing, are we? We're repurposing.' She pulled a taekwando pose, with her fists up in front of her face. 'We're garbage guzzlers!'

A hot wave of nervous dread rose up inside Laurie. She still couldn't believe her mum was getting them to do this, to be garbage guzzlers – people who eat discarded food from the bins of supermarkets, cafes and restaurants.

Laurie shook her head. 'And you're not even joking,' she said. 'That's the worst thing.'

'Wellies on, please, Lau,' said her mum.

Laurie couldn't believe this was happening. And to make matters worse, the whole thing was her fault. *Why* had she felt the need to show her family that documentary about food waste, when they already did *so much* to help save the planet? It had just convinced them they could do even more!

In the video, a guy who called himself 'Geoff the Garbage Chef' had been striding across a field, throwing potato peelings on to a barbecue, drinking sour milk straight from the bottle and talking about some chocolate biscuits he'd found in the supermarket bins.

'Open your eyes and fill your bellies!' he'd said. 'Because I've got a challenge for you. Can you go for a day, a week or how about an entire month, without buying food?'

Laurie cringed just thinking about it. Before the video

had even ended, her parents and Fern had signed up to the challenge. Dad had flung open the cupboards to dig out dusty lentils and broken spaghetti and Fern had found a recipe for the weirdest treacle tart ever, which used banana skins instead of pastry.

And now here they were, bin diving.

'There's no need to look so worried, Laurie,' said her mum. 'It's not a swimming pool. You don't actually have to *dive* into the bin.' She laughed. 'Just rummage around a bit and find us something nice to eat.'

Laurie's eyes flicked back to the mum and daughter in the jet-set jeans. Would they think that being a garbage guzzler, or a freegan, or a dumpster diver, or any of those other words that are used to describe people who eat the rubbish, was a criminal offence?

'Look, Mum, I know the supermarket has thrown the food in the bin but Dad says that strictly speaking it still belongs to them so it's illegal to—'

Laurie's mum waved her hands dismissively. 'Tell you what should be illegal, Laurie. Chucking out tons of bagels a week, that's what.'

'Wasting food is wrong,' said Laurie. 'I care about it too, you know! What I'm saying is, there are other ways to—'

Fern rapped on the back window. She squashed her nose, which was sprinkled in freckles like sesame seeds, up against the glass. 'Let's go.'

Laurie looked at Fern's bright hand-me-down pinafore. Sometimes she secretly wished she was nine years old again and that the mustard dress still belonged to her. She looked at the big heart-shaped patch on the skirt. Laurie had accidently torn the pinafore when she was climbing a tree, and her mum had patched it with a piece of fabric from one of Laurie's old Babygros.

She wouldn't have minded going into bins so much when she was Fern's age. *But I'm twelve now*, she told herself. *I'm not a kid any more.*

Laurie's face flushed. 'I'm not a pig, either,' she muttered out loud. Then she turned to her mum and said, 'That's what I'm saying. It's not just that I don't want to get into trouble. I don't want to eat out of bins. Full stop.'

Her mum snapped the glove compartment shut. 'I've found the head torch and the rubber gloves,' she said. 'And Fern's got the walkie-talkies. Right then, staying or coming, Laurie? Final decision.'

'Mum! Were you even listening to me?'

'Yes, Laurie. Oink, oink, oink.'

Mum scrunched up her nose and mouth. Her face was like elastic: she could stretch it into any expression she wanted. Laurie's teeth gritted as her mum started snorting around the dashboard. A bubble of laughter caught in Laurie's throat and she tried to turn it into a cough. The giggle burst out anyway.

'Come on,' said Mum. She opened the car door and stood next to Fern. 'Geoff the Garbage Chef says it's possible to find enough food in one bin dive for a family to eat for a week. When he gets that much, he calls it Garbage Gold! So it can't be hard to find a few extras . . .'

'Go for it, Laurie!' shouted Fern. 'Remember that

slogan from the video? *Garbage guzzling keeps the planet alive, so why not get your next meal from a dumpster dive!'*

Fern was so loud that people turned around and stared at them. Including the girl and her mum, who had finally freed a trolley.

It was Charley Keating-Sloss. Only the coolest, richest, most popular girl at school.

Laurie threw herself down in her seat. She yanked her cardigan right over her head, blood thumping with panic.

Had Charley seen her? Did she recognize her? Was she on her way over, ponytail a-swishing, to laugh at Laurie Larksie the Champion Dumpster Diver?

'What's going on?' said Mum.

Breathe, Laurie told herself. *Deep breath. Get a grip.* If Charley did come over (which was unlikely), all she'd see when she looked in the car was a pile of cardigan. There was no evidence they were going bin diving. Laurie could deny everything.

'Explain,' her Mum said.

'Don't look now but there's a girl from school,' said Laurie, her voice muffled. 'Over there with her mum and . . .'

Mum turned to look. 'What's wrong with that? We'd love to meet one of your friends. Go on, Lau, give her a wave.'

'No!' said Laurie, more sharply than she meant to. How could she explain to her mum that the thought of Charley – or 'Cha*rrr*-ley', as Charley herself pronounced it – meeting her family was terrifying?

Brainy, beautiful, with a breezy 'I-got-this' attitude and glossy hair that flowed over her shoulders like golden syrup, Charley Keating-Sloss paraded around Silverdale High School projecting the kind of confidence that comes with nailing the most important fashion decision of the year.

Laurie felt a tight squeezing feeling in her chest. If Charley saw her in her second-hand, recycled, hand-knitted clothes . . . She couldn't even finish the thought.

Her mum's voice lowered. 'I thought you said you

were getting on well with the others – that you'd made lots of new friends?'

'I have. I've told you about my best friends Zainab and Emilia. I'm in Year Seven, Mum! Charley's in Year Nine! I can't go and speak to someone like her.'

'Well, you've missed your chance now, anyway, there's no one beside the trolleys any more.'

Laurie slowly shifted up in her seat and peered through the material of her cardigan. Charley and her Mum had disappeared. So they hadn't seen her.

Yet.

Laurie was thinking fast. She was out of the danger zone for now. But how long would it be before Charley re-emerged? Twenty minutes, half an hour? Laurie looked at the bins. It was getting dark – she could be in and out of there in less than ten minutes.

Her head began to spin. Silverdale High was miles away from home. In fact, it was so far away from Pipson – the village where the Larksies lived – that no one else from Laurie's primary school had gone there. They were at the local secondary instead. And while Laurie did miss her old friends, she'd loved having a fresh start.

But no one at her new school, not even Emilia and Zainab, had ever met her family. No one knew how obsessed the Larksies were with recycling, reducing and repurposing. This year at Silverdale had been life-changing for her and she wasn't going to let her mum and Fern wreck everything. She wasn't going to turn into Garbage Girl!

She jumped out of the car.

'Oh, well done, love,' Mum patted her on the arm. 'We don't need much. Maybe some salady things. A pudding would be nice . . .'

'Give me the bags,' muttered Laurie, resigned, and with her cardigan over her head she sprinted to the bins.

The first bin was empty. The next one was stuffed with plastic. Laurie ripped the lid off the third and . . .

Jackpot!

The bin was so full of fresh, vibrant produce, it

looked like one of those earth bowls on Instagram. A bed of frilly lettuce leaves was piled high with fruit and vegetables, from red and yellow peppers to packets of diced butternut squash, and hundreds of bite-sized tomatoes, blueberries and raspberries.

With a surge of excitement, Laurie started stuffing the food into the bags. It was like an edible treasure trove! The sight of all that delicious food – just out here and free to take – drove any thought of embarrassment from her head. And as she dug deeper, it got even better. Cinnamon bagels, spicy bean sausages, yogurts, coleslaw and pizzas . . .

'Any celery or carrots?' Mum's voice suddenly came through the walkie-talkie. 'We could make dips with crudités.'

'It's OK, Mum,' Laurie said quickly. 'I've totally got this.'

Suddenly Laurie heard a noise – there were people going past the edge of the car park, not far from where she was. She ducked down behind the side of the bin and switched her head torch off.

There was chatter, laughter and a rattling sound, as if a can were being kicked along the road. *OK*, thought Laurie, *these people are just on their way to the bus stop or something*. She suddenly remembered about Charley, and started stuffing food in the bags faster than ever. Any minute now she would be back, and then . . .

She dug down into the next layer of the bin – it was full of puff-pastry rolls. She took a look at the price tag and was shocked at how much they cost. No wonder her parents never bought this stuff.

And there were jam doughnuts, biscuits, brownies . . . and a Peppa Pig birthday cake. Laurie grinned – Fern would think it was hysterical. She checked the back of the box. According to the best-before date, the cake didn't go off until midnight.

She grabbed the pizzas and bags of salad, fruit, biscuits and doughnuts and legged it back to the recycling area. She dumped the bags on the ground. 'First load beside the bottle bank,' Laurie hissed into the walkie-talkie. 'Over!' They'd agreed that her mum would collect them from there and put them in the car, but there was no sign of her.

'Be there in a sec,' said Mum.

When Laurie got back to the bins she spotted a crate lying around. She dragged it over and stood on it to get some extra height. Leaning in, she yanked a couple of plastic bags aside.

With her free hand, she pressed the TALK button on the walkie-talkie. 'Urggh!'

'What is it?' said Mum.

'Looks like someone's emptied a load of tomatoes underneath where the doughnuts were. I think it's pasta sauce or something.' Laurie re-angled the torch on her headband to get a proper look. Sticking out of the sauce was what looked like the humps of the Loch Ness Monster. 'No way! I can see mangoes!'

'Great! Let's do fruity puddings.'

'I was thinking hair conditioner! If you—'

'Don't tell me. Mash up mangoes and spread them on our heads?'

Laurie laughed. She and Fern loved making edible beauty products. It was their favourite thing ever. Using things they found in the kitchen, they whipped up lime and peppermint bath fizz, chocolate orange face masks, wild rose and strawberry moisturizer . . .

And they knew lots of tricks. Whenever Fern had been crying, say, Laurie would pop slices of raw potato over Fern's eyes and cheeks to reduce the puffiness. And once, when Laurie had a spot on her chin, they invented this serum – they called it 'Skin Whisperer' – made from tomatoes and it cleared up, really quickly.

'And post a photo of us . . .'

Laurie grinned. 'On Beauty in the Kitchen. Yes!'

That was the name of her account on School Stories, where only people at your own school could join your group and see your photos.

Laurie loved it. She'd only recently made her social media debut – she'd never had the confidence to post anything at her old school. But School Stories was different, and being in Year 7 was different too.

Now, whenever she and Fern had made a potion, they decorated them with rose petals or chocolate curls and posted the photos. And it had been amazing when a couple of people gave them a like or a share.

'May we have the mangoes?' Laurie asked through the walkie-talkie. 'Or one of them anyway?'

'Of course. Honestly, Lau, when you think of the farmers who grew them and the fact that the produce has been flown halfway round the world . . .'

But Laurie's head had spun off into how the mangoes would be brilliant for her vlog. As she leaned over the bin, throwing the fruit into bags, she imagined mashing up a mango, spreading it on Fern's head and having Fern swish her lovely glossy hair to the camera. Fern's hair was always shiny, but this would really give it some extra oomph. And she could finish the vlog by saying that it doesn't matter if you've not got a mango because it works with bananas and avocados too.

She grinned. This was going to be great. They'd get going on it tomorrow and . . .

Suddenly Laurie's eyes widened. Over in the far corner was the bright packaging of her favourite brand of nut butter. It cost a fortune – her Dad often said it would be cheaper to buy a hazel-tree orchard rather than another jar of it.

And it wasn't only a jar. The side of the crate said *500g tubs X 24*. Laurie did the maths. That single crate cost more than what the Larksies spent on groceries in a fortnight. Never mind a week.

This is it, thought Laurie. *This is #GarbageGold!*

If she managed to get that crate out of the bin, and if that crate really did contain those tubs, then BOOM! Her mum wouldn't make them go bin diving again because they'd have got so much in one go.

But she would need to get really close to it before she could lift it out – she knew it would weigh a ton. Laurie slowly looked around. She was starting to realize that she'd have to actually get into the bin to get the nut butter. She took another look at the sky. It was very late and she hoped that it was so dark no one would see her whether she got in or not.

Quickly she stood up on tiptoe, which was tricky in her wellies, grasped the side of the bin, swung her legs over and lowered herself into the rubbish. *Ha*, thought Laurie, *I suppose this is what you call a real bin dive!*

She knelt on a sack of potatoes and gently leaned forward, desperately trying not to slip in the garlicky pasta sauce.

Her mum's voice came through the walkie-talkie. 'We should probably get going now, Lau. Do you think you've got enough for the party?'

Laurie put her mouth to the receiver. 'Mum, I can't talk right now! I'm about to . . .' She broke off.

Leaning forward, Laurie shoved the walkie-talkie in her pocket, put her hands on either side of the crate and pulled. There was a nasty slurping noise, as if it were stuck to other things in the bin. She couldn't see much; the battery on her torch was low and the light was fading. With her hands around the crate, she slowly turned towards the side of the bin. She just needed to get it close enough to the side, so she could climb out of the bin, and then be able to easily reach it when she got out.

But the crate was so heavy that it slipped from Laurie's hands as she got it in position. With a thump it fell back into the bin. The second that happened, the sack underneath Laurie split, and the potatoes burst out.

It was like being in a ball pit where all the balls are mushy vegetables or doughnuts that are squashing beneath your feet, and you're falling further and further down. Laurie couldn't get a footing on anything, and in the panicky seconds that followed she toppled forward and fell splat into the pasta sauce.

'Aaarrrggghhh!' she yelled aloud.

Laurie flailed about for what felt like ages. In the end, she was forced to do a sort of breast-stroke action to wade through the discarded food. There was no way she was leaving the hazelnut butter, though. Not after all that. She threw it over the side of the bin, like sandbags out of a hot air balloon, and clambered out.

She strode back to her mum, who was by the car, pieces of mayonnaise-covered carrot and cabbage falling off her jeans.

'What happened? I thought I heard a shout but I wasn't sure if it was you.'

'Well, it was!' Laurie threw the crate of nut butter on the ground. 'I fell over, Mum, and it was absolutely disgusting . . . but it's over.'

Mum put her hand on Laurie's shoulder. 'Poor you. I've got some tissues in the car . . .'

Laurie pulled at her top – the pasta sauce was making her T-shirt stick to her skin. 'Did you hear me, Mum?'

'I think the whole car park heard you, Laurie.'

Laurie triumphantly held up a tub of hazelnut butter.

'Way to go, Lau!' said Mum. 'Is that what I think it is?'

'Garbage Gold!' said Laurie.

Laurie peeled her rubber gloves off – carefully, so she didn't drip any more bin juice on herself – and opened it. It was fudgy, thick and creamy. Even though she was covered in pasta sauce and bits of vegetables, she was also thinking about making hazelnut bites, with layers of chocolate, hazelnut butter and biscuit.

Suddenly Laurie started to shiver. Her wet T-shirt was making her cold in the night air. She didn't want to touch her clothes, so she gave herself a shake, trying to flick the food off. That released the smell even more.

'Urggh! I absolutely reek of garlic!'

Laurie suddenly felt tears prickling at the back of her eyes. The triumph of finding the hazelnut butter was quickly being replaced by the shock of falling over and swimming in rubbish. *Look at me: I'm a total, stinking MESS!*

'Come on, let's get you home,' said her mum. She put her arm around Laurie, and squeezed her tight. 'And into the bath before bed . . .'

Just then, Laurie caught sight of Fern. She was standing near the exit of the supermarket, making crosses with her fingers.

'Do you know what she's up to?' Mum tucked some

boxes of pizzas under her elbows. She looked like a duck with huge cardboard wings.

'Maybe she thinks I look like a vampire. Because I've got blood-red sauce down me.'

Laurie began a swaying walk. She wandered away from her mum and towards Fern, with her arms outstretched.

At that exact moment, Charley and her mother swung around the corner with their loaded trolley, and came face to face with Laurie.

CHAPTER TWO

Charley had seen her. Covered in bin juice and pretending to be a vampire. Laurie's heart was beating frantically. How was she going to explain this?

She could say that she was on her way to a fancy-dress party, as a zombie. That would explain the stupid walk. Laurie prayed that Charley wouldn't see the bags of food . . .

For a second she thought Charley was going to ignore her and follow her mum over to their car, which was parked behind where Laurie was standing. But then Charley did a double take, and raised her eyebrows.

'I'm sure I recognize you from school,' she said. She was sipping a fruit smoothie. 'Aren't you Laura someone?'

'*Lau*-reee! Can you help with the bags?' shouted Mum. 'I can't carry everything to the car by myself!'

Charley grinned. 'Well, *Lau*-reee. I'm Charley.'

Laurie nodded her head.

Charley was so vibrant and on-trend that it was hard to take your eyes off her. She was like a glittery, intergalactic bath bomb. Next to her, Laurie felt like a dreary bar of plain soap.

Charley flicked her ponytail. 'We're picking up snacks for a thing I'm having tomorrow.'

Laurie glanced over at Charley's mum, who was loading what looked like a month's worth of groceries into the back of their shiny sports car.

Laurie didn't know what to say. 'A thing?'

'You know, a few people are coming around.'

'Right.'

'For a party.' Charley looked over at her mum and waved. But Charley's mum didn't wave back.

She did another big swish of her ponytail.

'A *pool* party, actually. In our garden,' Charley said.

Laurie decided not to mention the zombie thing. Fancy dress sounded so babyish compared to a *pool* party.

Charley was looking at her appraisingly, eyes moving up and down. 'Soooooo,' she said. 'What happened to your clothes?'

'Oh, this?' Laurie's face flushed as she folded her arms to hide the worst of the tomato stains. 'It's nothing, I had a bit of accident with . . .'

Just then, Fern barged over, nearly knocking Laurie into Charley. 'We need help loading the car,' she said breathlessly. 'You did so well, Lau! You got loads of food for the Really, Really—'

'Wow, that's some outfit,' interrupted Charley, looking at Fern's brightly clashing mustard pinafore and indigo leggings.

Fern struck a pose.

Charley pointed her phone at her and there was a flash.

Laurie stared. No way was that OK!

'Please don't take photos of her,' said Laurie.

'Don't look so worried!' Charley laughed. 'I took it of her clothes, not her face.' She looked at Fern. 'I've got this School Stories account about fashion—'

'I love fashion so much!' interrupted Fern.

No. Just no, thought Laurie. *No! You cannot tell Charley Keating-Sloss that you make clothes out of old—*

'I made a dress the other day, out of a pillowcase, didn't I, Lau?'

Laurie wanted the earth to swallow her up.

Charley giggled. 'My account's called StyleFile.' She looked down at her phone. It looked like she was posting something.

Laurie's palms began to sweat. No way could Fern appear on that. StyleFile was full of photos of people's clothes – people Charley saw when she was out and about. Next to the picture, Charley listed where people had bought everything. But the Larksies didn't buy new things from shops, so Fern wouldn't be able to reel off a load of cool places their stuff came from, like everyone else did.

Laurie was panicking. Charley was going to ask Fern where she got her pinafore and leggings, and Charley would find out that they used to be Laurie's and that before that, her parents had got them free from . . .

Within seconds, Charley's phone was buzzing with likes on her StyleFile account. She turned the screen around. She hadn't lied about the photo; you couldn't see Fern's face.

Charley grinned. 'You're famous!'

Fern looked interested. 'How many followers do you have?'

'Six hundred and eighty-six on School Stories.' Charley's eyes sparkled.

Laurie forced herself to smile. 'That's over half the school.'

Fern grabbed Laurie's arm, her eyes dancing. 'Laurie's got a profile too! Do you follow her? She's called Beauty in the Kitchen and—'

'Don't!' said Laurie, sounding flustered.

'Oh yeah,' Charley said lazily. 'I heard something about that. Do you do those home-made beauty recipes or something?'

Laurie nodded.

Charley paused for a moment. 'Did you do the lemon drizzle lip sugar?'

'Yes.'

'And the gingerbread body lotion?'

Laurie smiled. 'That's one of our new ones, actually, but it works really well.'

Fern tapped Charley on the arm. 'I invent the recipes too. Did you see the blood orange bath fizz, last week? Oh! My! Gosh! You wouldn't believe how many orangey bubbles there were. In fact, we had to . . .'

Charley fixed her gaze on Laurie. Despite herself, she seemed interested. 'And they're made out of ingredients you find in the kitchen?'

With every nerve ending jangling, Laurie told Charley about the beauty treats they made, from ice-cream body scrubs to camomile tea cleansers. Laurie folded her arms over her wet T-shirt and forced herself to speak in an easy tone. 'This week, I even made an exfoliator with some old lentils that Dad found.'

'Don't forget to say about the packaging,' said Fern enthusiastically. She looked at Charley. 'We're totally plastic-free.'

'We collect things like walnut shells,' Laurie said quickly, cringing on the inside. 'And pour the lip balms into them, so everything is plant-based.'

Charley laughed. 'You are insane!'

There was an awkward silence.

Then Charley said thoughtfully, 'The thing is, though, it's not really about the number of followers or eating exfoliators. Is it? It's about the level of engagement and who endorses you.'

It was true that Charley got lots of engagement. Girls at school liked and replied to her every post. 'Oh Charley, that juice/dress/hat looks amaze!' or 'Where did you get it?' or 'Can I be on StyleFile next?'

Charley always replied in acronyms like '#Hats FTW YSK' or 'SLAP'. Some of them Laurie had to look up to find out what they meant. They were all confusing, FWIW.

'So,' said Fern, interested. 'Who endorses you?' She

said 'endorses' very carefully, and looked proud of herself for getting it right.

'Well, you know . . .'

'No, I don't,' said Fern genuinely.

Laurie took a deep breath. Everyone at Silverdale High knew about Charley's *celebrity endorsement*. But Fern was still at primary school. Charley launched into the story of how a minor royal had come to an event at her mum's work and somehow been shown her account and, apparently, been hugely impressed.

'And she said she wanted to follow me herself!' finished Charley.

Fern looked confused. 'But she can't, can she? Because she's not at your school.'

A swirl of what looked like annoyance flew over Charley's face. 'What she meant was—'

'Sorry,' said Laurie hastily. Her heart was racing. She couldn't believe that Fern had just insulted Charley Keating-Sloss like that. She was about to grab Fern and run when . . .

'These bags won't carry themselves!' Laurie's mum was coming towards them, arms flapping with boxes. 'Honestly, girls! I could do with some help.'

Charley's eyes widened. 'Someone likes pizza.'

'It's not for us,' Laurie said, thinking quickly. 'We're caterers . . .'

Mum dumped the food on the ground. 'That's over-egging it a bit, Lau,' she said, laughing. 'But I suppose we are in charge of the buffet.'

Charley smiled sweetly. 'Buffet?'

'There's a party on tomorrow at the Really, Really Free Market, in town,' said Laurie's mum.

A look of alarm shot across Laurie's face.

'The really, really *what*?'

'The Really, Really Free Market,' repeated Laurie's mum. 'You know, beside the canal.'

'Where everything's free,' said Fern. 'Clothes, tech, toys. I got my roller skates from there. And my bike.' She threw a biscuit into the air. 'Even the Wagon Wheels are free!'

'So sorry,' said Charley politely. 'I've never heard of it.'

And I never wanted you to, thought Laurie desperately. No one at school knew about the RRFM, let alone that Laurie went to it! And if Laurie was going to tell anyone, the *very* last person she would have told was super-shiny, most-popular-person-ever, Charley Keating-Sloss.

But her mum didn't know that. Laurie's heart pounded. The problem was, Charley didn't realize how different the Larksies were – how unusual it was to try not to spend money on anything.

Laurie felt her throat getting thicker. She was worried that if her mum mentioned the market again – or worse still, the pizzas – she would cry.

'It's wonderful!' Mum was saying. 'So many people, so much *sharing*! Clothes, bread, lampshades, you name it. We usually take our home-grown salads. But this week . . .'

Laurie's heart was racing.

'We need to get going!' she said quickly. 'Come on, Mum, Fern.'

Mum glanced at Laurie. 'Right, OK.' She heaved some bags up. 'Let's get all this stuff from the bins together.'

Charley looked puzzled. 'The stuff from the bins?'

Mum shook her head. 'Sorry, I meant the food!'

Laurie tugged urgently at Mum's sleeve. 'Let's go.'

Charley looked at Laurie's wet, stinky T-shirt and then at the bins, and then back at the piles of food that were lying there, some without bags.

The penny dropped.

'These pizzas are from the bins?' Charley said, her eyes popping wide open. 'They've gone off?'

There was a silence.

'No. They haven't gone off,' Laurie's mum said sensibly. 'This food is perfectly edible, you know.'

'Really?'

Laurie fixed her eyes on the ground.

'We must stop calling discarded food words like

"garbage" and "gone-off", just because it's in the bin,' continued her mum.

Laurie's cheeks were so hot she could have fried falafels on them.

Her mum rustled around in the bags. She found a doughnut. 'Look at this! Clean, fresh. In a wrapper.' She bit into it. 'Delicious!' she laughed. A blob of raspberry jam sat like a ruby on her lips, which were thickly coated in sugar.

Charley's mouth fell open.

Tears were gathering in Laurie's eyes. She couldn't believe her mum would go that far.

'Here, have the rest of the packet,' said her mum, holding the doughnuts out to Charley. 'This is all about sharing.'

Charley shook her head, looking absolutely appalled. 'I couldn't . . .'

Mum smiled. 'Or there's pizza?'

'That's a kind offer,' said Charley stiffly. 'But I'd better go.' Without even glancing back at Laurie, she dashed off to her mum's car.

As they drove home, Laurie sat very, very still and stayed very, very quiet. It was the only way to stop the tears from spilling over. That was literally the most rubbish experience of her life.

But the problem was, Monday might well be worse.

CHAPTER THREE

'Won't be a sec!' said Laurie. 'I'm going to get some herbs to put on the pizzas.'

It was Sunday, and nearly time for the RRFM party. Laurie's mum and Fern were rushing out to the car, arms full of pizzas, doughnuts and fruit. Her dad was in the kitchen.

'I won't be long either!' he shouted. 'Got to get these last few jars done.'

Laurie was in the hallway, pulling basil leaves off the walls.

The 'living' hallway was the first thing that anyone saw when they first arrived at Orchard End, and it was pretty wild. From the outside, the Larksies' house looked the same as the others in the row. A small Victorian cottage: faded brickwork, sash windows, and a magnolia tree in the garden. Inside, however, it was a high-tech, hydroponic growing farm and the entrance to this was the hallway.

Cherry tomatoes decorated the ceiling, like red fairy lights (they doubled up as baubles at Christmas), and rhubarb flourished in the darkness of what had once been the coat cupboard. Shelves of microgreens like watercress, pea shoots and spinach, lit with purple LED lights, were everywhere, like a living, leafy wallpaper.

The rest of the house was split into different growing zones. The sitting room bloomed with cherries and plums. There was a hedge along one side of the dining room bursting with blackcurrants and gooseberries. In the kitchen, there was a spectacular display of every salad leaf imaginable.

Upstairs was mainly exotic produce. There was a pineapple plant in the bathroom, kiwis on the landing, and lavender and lemongrass grew in the bedrooms.

To Laurie, it was home. And she was used to rattling off the explanation: how there was a global food crisis, why the science stacked up for growing food in affordable ways, without soil or natural light, how the Larksies had wanted an allotment but there were no plots available, so they'd thought, why not give this a go?

She caught sight of her reflection in the purple light of a glass tray full of plants. She had pulled her molasses-coloured hair into a chignon and tied it with a piece of material from the sewing box. She'd let some strands fall loose and thought it made her hazel eyes seem bigger and her face look older.

Despite the fact that she was still cringing every time she thought about the Charley-bin debacle – and she couldn't stop thinking about it – there were still some good things about the previous evening. She had struck Garbage Gold, which hopefully meant that her mum would never make them go bin diving ever again, and her dad had been made up to see the hazelnut butter. *That's a major plus*, thought Laurie, as she ran through the other things on her worry list.

The first and biggest problem was Charley. How could

she stop her from telling anyone that she saw them taking food from the bins? Loads of people who lived close by knew that her parents were very eco-friendly. And not in a cool, Instagram cashew cheesecake and vegan leather jackets way. She smiled. Her family was definitely more hippy than hipster. But no one at school knew how full-on anti-consumer they were.

She wished there was a sure-fire, water-tight, no-nonsense way do it. Like getting Charley to sign the Official Secrets Act to say she wouldn't tell anyone about her mum eating that doughnut. Laurie imagined sitting her down with some heavies from MI5 and insisting that garbage guzzling was an issue of national security.

Also, after last night's encounter in the car park, when Charley took that photo of Fern's clothes, Laurie had felt really bad. It's not that she wanted to have everything new and shiny, but it would be lovely to have even one outfit that they hadn't got for free, that she'd actually chosen, brand-new from a real shop. But how could she find a way to get some money to go to the shops without hurting her family's feelings?

'Lau! Can you give me a hand for a sec?' Dad shouted.

'OK!'

She went into the kitchen, where Dad was pouring home-made syrup into jars. It was his own recipe, an alternative to honey. It was giving off a warm, cheerful smell of vanilla and orange blossom. But Dad was in a mess; there were sticky puddles all over the counter.

'Let me do it.'

Quickly Laurie tipped the runny syrup from a little orange pan into the jars, screwed the lids on and put Dad's labels on the jars: *Hun-Knee, handmade by Ed Larksie.* She scribbled the date on them too.

'Thanks, Lau. Appreciated.'

Laurie looked at her dad. He was wearing jeans, which were creased and frayed along the bottom, and his DIY shoes: a scuffed old pair, splashed with paint.

'Great idea to add our own herbs to the pizzas,' her dad said, smiling. He put the jars in a box. 'Good one, Lau.'

She looked at the floor, which was made from reclaimed sustainable cork; the salad on the walls; the cabinet in the corner (which her mum had got for free from a sharing economy website), where her dad brewed kombucha, and where Fern's sourdough starter now bubbled and frothed; the piano on the far wall, which their neighbours had given them when they'd got a new one.

This place, Laurie thought, *it's not 'normal', is it?*

'Earth to Laurie!' Dad was waving his hands. 'Penny for them?'

'Talking of pennies, Dad, I was thinking about how I'd like to start buying things – you know, like clothes, and books and things. Instead of getting everything at the RRFM.'

Laurie's dad could sometimes be easier going than her mum, so it was worth a try.

His mouth dropped. 'Wow,' he said, gravely. 'Where's this coming from?'

'It's only money, Dad!'

He shook his head. 'Only money, eh?'

'I want to know what's so bad about going into town and, I don't know, getting a new top.'

Her dad looked like he'd been slapped across the face.

Laurie's cheeks went hot. 'Stop looking at me like I'm a criminal. It's not as if I've taken up vaping, or I've got a secret stash of plastic straws under my bed.' Laurie covered her hands with the sleeves of her top and folded her arms. 'I'm not saying I have to buy everything new and I don't want to take your money, or Mum's. I want to earn my own. I just don't want *everything* for free.'

'Kindness is free,' said her dad. He put his hand gently on her shoulder. 'And it's the only currency you need.'

Laurie sighed. 'No, Dad. Bitcoin is a currency. The euro is a currency, Sterling is a—'

Laurie and her dad jumped. It sounded like the front door was being bashed to bits. A second later, the letter box flew open. Fern's mouth was on the other side of it.

'Mum says that if you guys don't come right now,' yelled Fern, 'we're going to miss the cake! And it's the yummy meringue one that's made with leftover chickpea water.'

'Ever look at your wardrobe full of clothes and think, *I have nothing to wear*? Same. The Really, Really Free Market will cure you of that feeling,' shouted Romy. She gestured towards the rails full of dresses, skirts, jackets, trousers, jeans and T-shirts. 'So, come on over and help yourselves. Go crazy, people!'

Laurie squeezed through the crowd, carrying a tray. Romy was in her twenties and studying sustainable fashion at the local university, and she ran the clothes stall. She had a real knack for adding a fashion twist to the clothes collected from friends, skips and house clearances.

But Laurie reckoned even Romy probably bought stuff online or went to high street shops when she was twelve. It was OK, if you were older and cool like Romy, to wear old dresses from the 1990s, and jeans that you'd ripped yourself. But you couldn't be at high school and do that.

Thinking about fashion reminded Laurie of Charley. Quickly she swiped School Stories to see the StyleFile latest. No mention of pizzas, food waste or gifs of pigs in bins.

Just a three-way split between #friendship (selfies of Charley and her besties, Elise Roberts and Orla Hartford, in bikinis), #Party! (Charley bobbing about on a giant inflatable throne in her pool), and #Ice-cream (photos of three cones: cassis, lemon and pistachio).

I've got to switch off, Laurie told herself. *Stop obsessing. There's nothing I can do right now about Charley. I may as well enjoy myself.*

Laurie watched as Romy helped a woman try on lots of hats. She smiled. Romy was like the #OOTD app come to life. She could scan a person and a pile of clothes, and come up with the perfect Outfit of the Day in seconds. Just with her eyes.

Romy herself was rocking a 1960s fuchsia beret that she'd got on a clothes exchange app. She was telling the woman about her long search for a beret that fitted over her natural Afro curls. 'Since then, I've experimented with bucket hats, cloches,' said Romy. 'It's the quickest way to refresh your favourite outfit!'

She picked up a soft, metallic beanie and put it on the woman's head. The woman laughed and did a twirl. 'See, there you go,' said Romy. 'When you move it around, the threads catch the light. And it's free! Anyone else need some help?'

It wasn't only the clothes that people were buzzing around. The market was in full swing. The stalls, which ran along the canal towpath, were lit by a pretty string of fairy lights which glowed in the dusk, and the place was ablaze with chatter and music – a band called Upcycled Ukuleles was playing.

People were trying on hats, and looking at crockery, make-up, bikes, stereos, chairs, lamps, books, bread, cakes and cardamom knots, and the world's greatest chocolate vegan meringue pie, available on the 'Aquafaba-tastic' stall, and Laurie's heart did a little flutter as she remembered they'd be eating that later.

Fern waved a spicy bean sausage in front of Laurie's face. 'By the way, while we were waiting for you in the car, I had a jig round the pizzas. I've done faces on them with the sausages. Does this look like Dad's nose or what?'

Laurie laughed. 'Fern, you can't say that!'

Just then there was a cheer from the tech stand, a few stalls away from where they were standing. Fern dashed off to investigate and came back a moment later, saying that Radzi was back from his conference in Asia, and he was demoing a prototype of a skyscraper covered with coffee plants.

Radzi! Laurie felt a surge of happiness. Radzi was the Larksies' lodger and he was living with them while he studied for a PhD in urban agriculture. The arrangement had only been meant to last for a year – Laurie's parents had advertised for a student lodger because they needed the money, and for Radzi, living with a family who had pineapples in the bathroom was dream accommodation. That was three years ago. Radzi had never left, and no one wanted him to.

'Says he's going to solve the global coffee crisis,' said Fern, her arms waving about in excitement.

Laurie looked at Fern's little face. Most nine-year-olds spend time on games consoles, tablets, smartphones – but neither of them had been allowed screen time. Laurie had wanted to do those things, but not Fern. She never asked to go online, didn't use her smartphone much, and couldn't care less that the Larksies didn't subscribe to TV streaming services.

Fern's mind was on the pizzas again. 'On some pizzas, I've used Wagon Wheels for eyes,' she added seriously. She grinned. 'I've put the best one at the bottom of the tray, so you and me can share it later.'

'Awesome,' said Laurie.

Laurie, Fern and their parents handed out the pizza and puddings as they walked through the market. Finally they gathered around Radzi's self-watering coffee farm skyscraper. 'This system uses only two per cent of the water of a conventional coffee plantation,' said Radzi.

'What a time to be alive,' said Dad.

Mum put her arm around Laurie. 'Your hair looks lovely, by the way.'

'Thanks.'

But the mention of her hair had turned Laurie's mind back to Charley and the events of the previous evening. *The thing about money*, thought Laurie, *was how do you get it, when you're twelve?* She thought about the times she'd ever handled cash. Basically, it was only ever when she was fundraising for charity. She remembered the book sales she and Fern had done and about that time they 'invented' iced water and sold it to the neighbours, in aid of the sea turtles.

She couldn't go around fundraising for herself though. She pictured herself knocking on doors. *'Hello, I'm collecting for Laurie Larksie . . .'*

It was a fun thought. Laurie pictured a promo, like

the little clips on social media when there's an appeal on. She imagined people in an office, dashing around helping others, her favourite songs playing in the background.

In her head a phone was ringing. A cheery voice would answer and say something like: *'Hello, this is the RSBCLL, the Royal Society for Buying Clothes for Laurie Larksie . . .'*

She giggled. *It's not funny really*, she thought, quickly, with a pang of guilt. *I've got lovely clothes, and a safe warm home.* She knew her dad would say it should really be Laurie in the RSBCLL office raising money for others, not for herself.

Her brain suddenly snapped back into focus, as her phone was going off in real life. It was a message from Zainab. She'd taken a selfie, sitting on a hay bale, waiting for a foal to be born (her mum was a vet and Zainab and her little brother had to go with her when she was on call at the weekends). Laurie sent a load of supportive emojis.

'And it's as simple as that.'

Laurie looked up.

'Great work!' Radzi was nodding encouragingly at Fern, who was dripping water from a complicated-looking set of pipes on the model skyscraper.

Laurie's dad checked his watch. 'We should get going. It's nearly past my bedtime.'

'Cake first,' said her mum. 'Here she comes! Gosh, to think that it's one year today since Marika founded the RRFM.'

Marika, a woman in her seventies in a long, flowing smock with short-back-and-sides grey hair and a gravelly voice, was walking towards them. She was carrying an enormous chocolate meringue pie with one candle on it. A crowd of stallholders and customers gathered around.

'Happy Birthday to you,' crooned Marika.

Everyone joined in and sang Happy Birthday to the RRFM. Then Marika bent down and nodded at Fern, who blew the candle out. There was a cheer as Marika sliced the pie, and people were laughing and chatting and mentioning the best thing they'd ever found at the market.

The pie had a crisp, chewy cocoa meringue base and it was filled with hazelnuts and chocolate drops and piled with coconut cream and glistening crimson raspberries.

Fern leaned over and whispered in Laurie's ear. 'Obviously, it doesn't taste anything like as nice as that Peppa Pig cake you got.'

Laurie giggled. In fact, the meringue was one of the nicest things Laurie had ever eaten. She licked the cream from her fork and wondered if it was rude to ask for another slice. But then all the sweetness went out of her mouth.

'Listen to this, Larksies!' her mum was saying. She put her arms around Laurie, Fern, Radzi and Laurie's dad, and pulled them close together, as if they were in a rugby scrum. 'Marika says everyone's been blown away with how much food you got, Lau, and I agree with her. Why stop here?'

Laurie's stomach started to spin with anxiety.

Marika had suggested the Larksies give away food from the bins at the March 4 Climate in town next month. The Larksies had already decided to go on the march (in fact, Fern had started to plan her costume). According to Marika, there would be lots of people there who cared about food waste but didn't realize how much food was being thrown out. Handing out from the bins would be very powerful, she said.

'It will give us a chance to really engage with people,' Laurie's mum went on. 'The RRFM is great but everything's free here . . .'

'Great idea!' said her dad. 'Must say, the pizzas and puds have gone down a treat today.'

'We'll hand out free doughnuts and apples!' said Fern. She began to march on the spot.

Laurie's mum continued 'And when we tell them we found the food in the bins, I think everyone will be disgusted.'

'Exactly!' said Laurie, her face flushed. 'Totally disgusted.'

Her mum laughed. 'Oh, Lau.' She put her hand on Laurie's shoulder. 'I meant because of the waste.'

'It'll be like other food waste cafes,' said her dad. 'Like that one in Leeds, which makes great sarnies and soups.'

'People will soon stop being disgusted when they realize everything is free,' said Fern reasonably. She squeezed Laurie's arm. 'That's true, isn't it, Lau? Who in the world does not like free doughnuts?'

'Never a truer word was spoken,' said their dad.

Imagine if anyone from school saw them; last night had been bad enough! Laurie's pulse started beating wildly. She had to get out of this! She felt bad, knowing it was a really important issue, but she didn't want people to *associate* her with bin food.

'What are you thinking, Lau?' asked Dad encouragingly.

I'm thinking this is a nightmare! Her stomach lurched. *But what I'm also thinking is that I must stay positive.*

She took a deep breath and did her best to smile. 'Sounds like a plan.'

Chapter Four

First thing on Monday morning it was Lower School assembly. Laurie, Emilia, Zainab and the rest of their form trooped down to the school hall. They were sitting in the chairs near the front, squashed in with the rest of the Year 7s, with the rows of Year 8s and 9s filling up the rest of the hall.

Now that it was summer term, Laurie found school far less daunting than she had back in September. And being such good friends with Emilia and Zainab had really helped her to settle in.

Occasionally, though, Silverdale High could still feel new and overwhelming. There were all of those endless corridors, and new subjects like DT, ICT and Rugby to get used to. And the hectic lesson changes, when older pupils often pushed past the younger ones, could feel quite unnerving.

At primary, they'd stayed in the same little classroom all day.

Don't think about it, Laurie told herself. She had a sudden pang to be back safe and warm in Mrs Burgess's class, doing something lovely. Like that time they'd made clay pots for their Greek project.

Forget it! Think of the brilliant things about Silverdale High . . . like the tights! thought Laurie, looking at her knees. They made her legs look silky, longer and older.

After years of wearing tights made from reclaimed wool (her mum bought them online from a business on a Scottish island, which unravelled old knitwear and turned them into tights so thick and itchy they were basically jumpers in the shape of tights), she was finally in black 60 denier, like all the other girls.

It was such a relief!

It was OK to roll out of bed, stick on fluffy tights and head out to primary school, thought Laurie, looking like you're wearing a sheep costume on your legs – like Fern does – but you couldn't go to *this* school and do that.

Mrs Kapoor, the head teacher, appeared on the stage. She pulled the sides of her jacket together, and smiled. 'I have an important announcement this morning, which I'm delighted to say—'

'Hey! You there at the back!'

Everyone's head whipped around.

'Turn that phone off now!' Mr Bakala, the Maths teacher, roared. He pointed at a red-faced boy in Year 9. 'This is assembly, not a call centre!'

As Mr Bakala told him off in front of everyone, Laurie spotted Charley – front and centre of the first row of Year 9s.

Charley was wearing her tie over her jumper – *fashion risk of the day*, thought Laurie – and she had a double-twisted ponytail. Two strands of hair on each side had been looped into a ponytail, giving her a carefree, laid-back look. She was a fabulous example of how versatile school uniform can really be. From her loosely knotted tie to her clingy jumper, she was an endless source of fashion inspiration.

Laurie tried to work out her expression. It was hard to analyse it from such a distance, and it wasn't as if Charley were looking in her direction. Even, so, Laurie's brain began to churn out anxious thoughts.

'Final warning, everyone!' said Mr Bakala. 'If I hear another ringtone, that's it.'

'As I was trying to say,' Mrs Kapoor went on, sounded irritated. 'Some of you may have heard of an entrepreneur scheme running in local schools called "The Disruptors". Similar to a programme called *Young! Talented! Rich!* is how it's being described, I believe.'

A buzz of anticipation broke out across the hall.

'Well, I'm delighted to tell you that Silverdale High is going to take part.'

Laurie didn't watch *Young! Talented! Rich!* but she knew the basic concept: you had to start a business and make as much profit as you could, and the person who made the most money was the winner.

Money!

Laurie's heart skipped. *This is it*, she thought. *This is the answer to everything*. The words 'Laurie Larksie, entrepreneur extraordinaire' flashed across her mind, like they were written in fireworks.

'This is a school-wide competition,' said Mrs Kapoor. 'You've got one month and a start-up loan of ten pounds.' She waved a wad of notes. 'I'll be giving these out as soon as you've sorted yourselves into teams. You'll need to create a product or service, learn about marketing and sales . . .'

Another phone went off.

'Right!' yelled Mr Bakala at a girl in Year 8, who rolled her eyes. He marched over to where she was sitting, near the back, and held his hand out for it. 'You know the rules – you can't collect your phone from the office until you've spent a lunchtime on litter-picking duty. But if it happens again, there will be a phone call home to your parents. And I'll be the one making it.'

While all this was going on, Laurie could hear the excited buzz of tons of ideas being unleashed. Jessica

Higgins, the Year 8 girls' football captain, said she might sell training sessions; Lexi Thomas, editor of the school magazine, was talking about charging people for managing their social media. Some boys in Year 9 were up for getting on their bikes and offering a courier service. Others were talking about everything from printing T-shirts to running coding workshops for older people to holding starry night camping events.

Emilia gave Laurie a friendly shove. 'Are you listening? This sounds good.'

Laurie snapped back to reality. 'What?'

'Not Bakala!' Emilia laughed. She tucked her knees up on the chair. Emilia was very small, and when she did this she was so compact that she looked like a little origami of a person. 'I meant the programme!'

'It sounds awesome,' said Zainab. She brushed away a strand of her shiny black hair as she leaned over to speak to them. Her eyes were bright and intense. 'Are you free to come to the cafe after school? We need a meeting about the business we're going to run.'

'Defo.' Emilia clutched her stomach. 'I'm so hungry, today I'm going to buy a chocolate brownie. Or two!' She nudged Laurie again. 'Coming?'

Laurie bit her lip. 'Oh, I'd love to but—'

Zainab's face fell. 'Don't say you have to go straight home. Again.'

'They do your favourite cake now: dairy-free lemon drizzle,' said Emilia, crossing her legs over. 'Just saying!'

'Yes, they do! I saw it too,' said Zainab, excited. 'And I read the ingredients list for you to check there were no eggs or anything. So, you *can* eat something there, after all.'

Laurie forced a smile. 'It's not that, it's—'

'It's squidgy and sugary and it's got syrup as well as icing. You should see how thick the icing is.' Emilia held her fingers about three inches apart.

Laurie pulled her bag on to her lap. When the other two weren't looking, she ducked her head into the bag and opened her purse. Had she mysteriously come into some cash? As if. The only thing she had was the

Emergency Fiver. Not to be spent without good reason, her mum said.

Mrs Kapoor clapped her hands. 'Listen up, please.'

She ran through the rules: teams had three weeks to sell as many products as possible and there would be a school sale event for the final weekend, so everyone's family and friends could come along and support them.

And as for the money, once each team had repaid the initial ten pounds, Mrs Kapoor explained that it was up to them to decide how to use the profits. 'Unless of course you've made hundreds.' She laughed. 'In which case, we'll talk about making a donation to the school, and in return for those donations we'll name a new Science lab after you, or put your name on a plaque in the school library!'

Laurie decided that she would give nearly all of the money away, but keep a few pounds so she could go to the cafe with the others. She grinned. That would be so cool! She'd march straight up to the counter, and tell Zainab and Emilia they could order anything they want. 'It's on me!' she pictured herself saying, her arms outstretched.

And she wouldn't forget Fern. She would buy cakes to take home for her. And hot chocolate. *In fact, why not take Fern to the cafe itself?* thought Laurie excitedly.

Other local schools were taking part too, explained Mrs Kapoor. This meant that there would be a winner in each school. But there would also be an overall winner: not necessarily the team who had made the most profit, but the team that had demonstrated the most innovation and creativity with their business idea.

And the judges, said Mrs Kapoor, were Amy and Avril Delamere. Still in their twenties, the Delamere sisters were not only founders of a super-cool brand of trainers, but they were hands down the most well-known and successful people to have ever been to Silverdale High.

Another ripple of excitement went around the room.

'And it goes without saying that I'd very much like Silverdale High to win,' said Mrs Kapoor. 'The prize for the winning school is a new 4D printer, which can print everything, from biscuits to parts of bikes. You'll all have a chance to use it in Design Tech lessons! And the winner and their class also gets to go on a "You're the CEO" day, finding out what it takes to run the company of your dreams.'

The room exploded into gasps and cheers.

Mrs Kapoor went on to tell them that if, for example, your business idea was selling ice cream, perhaps you'd go to an ice-cream factory and learn how to mix up new flavours. Or if you were doing fitness training, you could meet up with a free runner.

Emilia's hands were gesturing wildly. She was so animated she was breaking out into Polish – which she did every time her bakes came out best in Food Tech. She nearly knocked Zainab's glasses flying. Not that Zainab seemed to mind. She had already taken a notepad and pen out of her bag in case inspiration hit her before they even left the hall.

Mrs Kapoor raised her arm for silence. 'So, listen carefully. The theme for the competition is as follows: *If I could invent one thing to make the world a better place . . .*'

CHAPTER FIVE

'The lemon drizzle is this way!' said Zainab and Emilia as they steered Laurie through the school gates and towards the cafe, instead of the bus stop.

The day had flown by. Every lesson had been taken up with the competition, from ideas of what to do to how to spend the cash. Teachers had been helping with equipment and some super-organized people had already collected their start-up money.

Laurie pulled her phone out. 'I'll text Mum to say I'll be late.'

'Well, don't tell her you're texting and walking at the same time,' joked Zainab. 'What did you say she thinks that's called?'

'Wexting!'

Emilia laughed. 'I still can't believe we haven't met

your mum and dad, by the way.'

'You've got to invite us home soon,' said Zainab, in her slightly bossy voice. 'You've been to ours, and we've heard so much about Fern, and Radzi. We'd love to meet them in real life!'

'Mmm,' said Laurie non-committally. 'Shame it's so far away . . .'

That had been Laurie's excuse all year. Zainab and Emilia both lived within walking distance from school, in the same suburb. They walked home together each day, while Laurie had a long bus ride through country lanes, back to Pipson.

'I'll get us a table,' said Laurie as they arrived. 'I'm not hungry.'

Emilia touched her arm. 'Sure?'

'Honestly! I'm still full of lunch.' Laurie flashed them a smile. 'You saw the buckwheat pancakes.'

Zainab dropped her voice to a whisper. 'Because we can lend you some money if you've forgotten your purse again.'

'It's not that! I'm totally stuffed from lunch,' said Laurie, as cheerfully as she could.

Laurie knew they were trying to make her feel better. And Emilia and Zainab's kindness was part of why she loved being BFFs with them. But it was also why she often felt so embarrassed.

'Thinking about it, it's my turn to get the hot chocolates,' said Zainab, opening her purse. 'Cacao is healthy. It's full of antioxidants, iron and magnesium.'

'And I'll get the cake in.' Emilia pulled out a note. 'Packed with energy.'

Laurie shook her head. 'Thanks, but no need!' She picked up the jug of tap water. 'You know me! I love my H_2O.'

She'd never have thought pretending to prefer cold water to hot chocolate was going to be such a big part of being in high school.

'Well, if you're sure . . .' said Zainab, exchanging a look with Emilia.

Laurie put her hands to her cheeks. She felt as hot

and red as the cherries on the Bakewell tarts on the counter. 'Totally! You get in the queue.'

Why am I here? Laurie asked herself. Just because they were best friends didn't mean that she'd had to come to the cafe! She looked around, taking in the old-fashioned wooden tables with old treacle tins filled with brown sugar on them, and chairs and sofas scattered with pink marshmallow-coloured cushions. Kids were lounging on the sofas, tapping away on their phones, talking and eating cake. Finally Laurie spotted an empty table, squashed next to the wall.

It was near to Annie Brooks and Zoe Fitzgerald, two girls in her year. They were drinking hot chocolate and laughing. Laurie could tell they weren't laughing at her or anyone else but something funny about school, or life or whatever.

Annie caught her eye and gave her a wave. Annie was lovely. She had big green eyes, did quick, squirrel-like movements, and she was very emotional. If she wasn't giggling, she was sobbing on Zoe's shoulder about her

67

latest crush and Zoe *never* seemed to get annoyed.

Crushes!

That was another new thing. At primary school you could get away with saying you were crushing on a YouTube celeb or whatever. But now, you had to crush on somebody at school, and be in a School Stories messaging group with them and everything. Talk about pressure!

'Hi, Laurie!'

Laurie flushed. It was one of her form mates, Elliot Harvey. Elliot was short, stocky and inquisitive, and he kept a long, flat pebble, like an insole, inside one of his shoes, which meant he walked slightly awkwardly.

He was conducting an erosion experiment. Elliot weighed the pebble every six months to see how quickly the sweat was wearing it down. Laurie found it pretty gross.

He adjusted his glasses. 'What d'ya get in the Music assessment?'

Laurie did an eye roll.

Elliot was friendly, easier to talk to than most boys, but very competitive. He and Laurie had recently come joint second in the Science assessment, with 91 per cent. And not beating Laurie seemed to be a bigger deal to Elliot than losing out to Zainab's 95 per cent top place.

'Eighty-nine per cent,' said Laurie.

Elliot's face fell. 'I got eighty-seven per cent.'

'That's good.'

'Only a mark in it, really.'

'Hmm.'

'The others let me down in the practical,' said Elliot thoughtfully. He wiped his glasses. 'I was trying to direct them, with that piece I composed. And I'm not saying it was their fault or that Mrs Norton is biased but . . .' He shook his head. 'Hopeless!'

'Sure.' *Like it mattered*, thought Laurie. She didn't know why Elliot was so keen to beat her all the time. 'It was only a Music assessment.'

'Elliot turned his phone around and showed Laurie the language app he was using to revise for the Spanish assessment later that week. For a minute or two they had fun testing each other on the words for colours.

Elliot flicked it off. 'Get ready to be beaten!'

Laurie shrugged. 'Whatever.'

She sat down at the free table and her eyes flicked over to the counter, where the lemon cake caught her eye. Em wasn't wrong. It was thickly iced, luscious and dripping in syrup. Laurie's stomach flipped. Then she caught Emilia's eye and looked quickly away, worried that Emilia had seen her slobbering like a dog. Had the others seen her too? Laurie slid down in her seat and hid her face behind a menu.

OK. Relax, Laurie told herself. She started reading the menu, noticing that a lot of the options had a vegan sign.

She was thinking that when she finally earned some money she should buy some of the plant-based wraps, because if no one bought these things, the cafe would take it off their menu – and then what? Her parents would accuse them of not catering for plant-based diets. She giggled as she imagined her family starting a new campaign: Save the Spinach and Falafel Wrap!

'What are you laughing about?' said Zainab, sitting down.

'Nothing.'

Emilia plonked a plate of lemon drizzle on the table. 'Looks loads nicer than brownies, and this is my shout – no arguments, you two!'

Zainab smiled at Laurie. 'We know it's your favourite.' She handed out the forks and started eating one of the slices in small, very tidy bites.

An odd feeling shot straight through Laurie. Emilia and Zainab were so kind, but she didn't want them to buy lemon drizzle instead of the brownies they'd been longing for all day. *What is this?* she thought sadly. *The Royal Society for Buying Laurie Larksie's Favourite Cake?*

'Thanks so much,' said Laurie. 'The cake is perfect.'

Emilia wiped some sugar off her lips. 'What shall we do, then? For the competition?'

'I had an idea, actually.' Zainab's voice was rising in excitement. 'You know how everyone asks to copy my work?'

Emilia pulled a face. 'Don't tell me this is about homework.'

'I thought I could run a breakfast study club!' said Zainab. 'In the library, before school, where I help people with their homework. The library is deserted at that time and . . .' She looked at them both. 'What?'

'It's a great idea,' said Laurie, with an encouraging smile. 'And there's definitely a need for it. Personally, I hate homework, but . . .'

Emilia waved her fork in the air. 'It's not really right for this, Zain.'

Zainab brushed away a strand of her espresso-coloured hair. 'But it fits the "one thing to make the world a better place" theme, because if everyone achieved their targets at school—'

'We need to give people what they want,' said Emilia. 'And no one wants extra study. I'm sorry, Zain. If you were going to achieve other people's targets for them, that might be a goer, in fact, I can see that working . . .'

'That's cheating,' Zainab said, sounding grumpy. She

scooped up a dollop of lemon icing. 'And don't gang up on me. You know I don't like it when you do that.'

Laurie knew Zainab well enough by now to know that when she started on a bad idea you had to quickly replace it with a better one without hurting her feelings. Otherwise she'd go on and on . . .

'It's a great start,' said Laurie quickly. 'And if it was me, Zain, I'd go for it.'

'Thanks, Laurie. But you usually do better than me anyway.'

Emilia was getting animated. 'We need a product that everyone wants, we need to appeal to . . .' She swivelled around as the cafe door swung open. 'People like her, for example.'

Laurie looked up and felt a deep chill. Charley stood framed in the entrance of the cafe. Sweating and sparkling in her PE kit, she exuded super-fit radiance and power like an inspirational wellness vlogger. It was a real up-switch in energy from Saturday's car park appearance, and Laurie couldn't take her eyes off her.

She shivered. In the excitement of the competition she had barely thought about the mortifying events of Saturday evening.

Emilia dropped her voice to a whisper. 'Anyone who could sell to the popular girls, and best of all to Charley Keating-Sloss, would win for sure.'

'What's she staring at?' said Zainab.

Laurie's pulse quickened. She was absolutely kicking herself that she'd come to the cafe. Charley had probably forgotten all about her, but now here she was, staring Laurie full in the face. Probably thinking about gone-off pizzas and doughnuts . . .

'She's coming over!' Emilia looked surprised.

Laurie stuffed an ice cube into her mouth. *Here it comes*, she thought. *Show time.*

'Can you join me, Laurie?' Charley tipped her head towards the table next to the window.

Zainab gave her a startled glance, which made Laurie feel even more uncomfortable.

'Sure.'

Laurie told herself not to panic. All she needed to do was tell Charley that the bin diving had been a real one-off, and there was no need to mention it to anyone. Ever. If she was polite and quick, she would be back at the table with Zain and Emilia asap.

'Bring your drink?'

Laurie's eyes flicked to her glass. There was no way she could drink free tap water in front of Charley. Her brain clanged loudly.

'I was about to get a hot chocolate,' she said.

Zainab and Emilia threw her a confused look.

Laurie's hand shot into her bag for the fiver. If this wasn't an emergency, what was?

CHAPTER SIX

Weirdest. Conversation. Ever.

'I'll get straight to the point.' Charley leaned forward in her seat. 'I love the idea of your home-made beauty products.'

Laurie nearly spat out her hot chocolate. That was not what she was expecting Charley to say to her, sitting in the cafe after school only two days after she had seen her taking pizzas from the supermarket bins. She stared at Charley, desperately trying to find a string of words that would somehow pass as a reply.

Charley did a tinkly laugh. 'Your face! But yes, I'm serious. I know a winning product when I see one.' She swiped her phone. Laurie couldn't see what she was looking at, but Charley was smiling at the screen.

Laurie wiped her mouth. 'Which one?'

'LOL!' said Charley. 'You're funny. But you know what?' She pointed at Laurie. 'You're right. They're all totally awesome.'

Laurie still felt confused. 'You mean my Beauty in the Kitchen stuff?'

'Of course I mean Beauty in the Kitchen! Though I do think that name sucks. No one wants their face to look like a fridge-freezer. The thing is, edible beauty is so in right now,' Charley said. She picked up the tin of sugar, which was on the table, and used it as a dumb-bell to tone her arms. 'And as that's your brand identity, I can see these products working.'

What? She and Fern didn't want to put nasty chemicals on their skin, so they made potions from whatever was in the kitchen. But that's not a 'brand identity'. Surely that was just her and Fern dolloping yogurt on their faces . . .

Laurie sniffed her wrist. She'd put some home-made blackcurrant crumble body oil on herself that morning. The scent reminded her of home, and helped her feel calmer.

'Didn't you say you used nutshells for packaging? Love it! My dad says that retailers are getting a really hard time about plastic, now everyone's gone all climate-changey. So, your ideas are very zeitgeist. May I smell?'

Laurie held her arm out, and as Charley breathed in the scent, a strand of Charley's hair fell on to her arm. Laurie felt her scalp tingle and the tickly feeling trickled down to her shoulders and her spine. It made her toes go funny. 'The scent comes from the blackcurrant leaves, which means you can wear the perfume without getting your wrists stained.'

'Seen it,' said Charley. 'It's one of those Puddings Perfumes you make, isn't it? Don't look so surprised.' She waved her phone. 'I've been watching your vlogs!' She laughed. 'It sounds like straight-up witchcraft the way you go on about the eco ingredients. But I like that you know so much.' She flashed a smile. 'When I'm Prime Minister I'm going to introduce a law: the study of beauty will be a compulsory GCSE. So what do you think?'

'That you'll get top marks.' The words were out before Laurie could stop them. She felt her face colouring into a massive red-cheeked emoji.

Charley glanced appreciatively at her reflection in the cafe window. 'I meant about teaming up for The Disruptors. What do you think?'

'You and me?'

Laurie felt like she'd swallowed some fiery ginger cordial and it was rushing and burning down into her chest. *Charley Keating-Sloss wants me to work with her for the competition?* Her head whizzed with possibilities.

Charley whacked her smile up to full beam. 'Look, I can't make you team up with me. If you can't stand the idea, that's your lookout. You'll be going around thinking, *Ooh, imagine what it would have been like to win The Disruptors, to be a beauty entrepreneur. . .*'

An image shot through Laurie's mind of stepping on to the stage at the front of the school hall as the winner.

'. . . but too late!' said Charley. 'I'll only ask you once.'

Laurie pulled her school jumper over her hands and

scrunched the material between her fingers. She was worrying about what Emilia and Zainab would think.

They hadn't technically decided to be a team, but Laurie felt like Emilia had been about to suggest something.

And what about Fern? They'd always made the recipes together. Laurie couldn't go off and sell them! Could she?

Charley leaned back, with her hands behind her head. 'Now, I'm not trying to rush you . . .'

'Thanks,' said Laurie.

'But we do have to decide today.'

Laurie heard a scraping of chairs. Zainab and Emilia were putting on their coats. Zainab mouthed *Call us later*, and they both waved goodbye.

Charley sighed as though she had years' worth of experience of running a successful global business. 'Take it from me, Laurie, besties don't make the best business partners.'

Laurie threw back her drink. It was sweet and sludgy. She wished she'd stuck with the water.

Charley continued briskly. 'Words like "influencer" are one hundred per cent cringeworthy but we both know what I mean.' She leaned her elbows on the table and looked sincere. 'The truth is, I'll love using your products on my face and you'll love using my face for your products!'

She's right, thought Laurie. Charley was talented, popular, on-trend and top of her class in everything, so whatever she got behind was bound to win. And if she wore Beauty in the Kitchen products . . .

'There! Decision made,' said Charley.

'What?'

'I've signed us up.'

Charley's thumbs were drumming away on her phone screen. 'I've put "food waste" as our make-the-world-a-better-place thingy. And that if we win, I've said we want to take everyone to our favourite beauty company HQ, for a You're the CEO of Bubble Bars day.'

'That's completely my dream!' blurted out Laurie. 'Like forever!'

Her mind threw up a vision of a spellbinding place, a bit like a spa, a bit like a lab, but much cooler than both. A place bursting with sherbet lemon bath fizzes, jars of jellies, waterfalls of glitter, strawberries, chocolate, caramel, vanilla and cream . . .

'It's loads of people's dream, Laurie,' said Charley, with a sophisticated wave of her hand.

She pulled her PE fleece over her head and let down her hair. The double twists unravelled into a tumble of relaxed, mermaid waves, which suited her ethereal beauty. 'But together, you and I could actually make it happen.'

Laurie took a deep breath. 'Do you really think we could win?' she said, suddenly. 'That people would actually buy our products?'

'They'd be mad not to,' Charley said with a grin.

Chapter Seven

Two minutes later Laurie was outside the cafe, full of worry. She knew that she needed to tell Emilia and Zainab straight away or she wouldn't be able to concentrate on anything else.

She looked at her phone. As usual, there was a ton of messages on the Year 7 group chat on School Stories. There was a row about who hid the whisks they'd needed in Food Technology (which had led to very lumpy pancakes), and Harry Evans, who was a conspiracy theorist, was putting it around that the cheese paninis in the canteen were made of rubber. But Laurie skipped straight to the direct messages from Zainab and Emilia.

@Zainab What was that about? Hope you're OK x

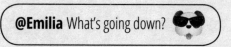

@Emilia What's going down?

She didn't know what to tell them. Rain was falling on Laurie's screen, so she stuffed her phone in her bag.

She was at the bus stop later than usual and there was hardly anyone around. She was the only one who went right to the end of the line on the number 3, but there were usually other kids on there at the start, being dropped off along the way.

Laurie decided that she would video chat with Emilia and Zainab on the bus. It would help the time to speed past. Plus, it was too hard to hold her phone and the umbrella.

But then the bus was packed, and Laurie spent the journey squashed next to a mum with a toddler who was screaming because he dropped his snack on the floor. Which meant Laurie was nearly home before she made the call.

She stopped beside the edge of the lane, under the trees. At Laurie's feet there were new fern leaves unfurling their golden green spirals, and above her, yellow catkins were hanging from the branches of the trees in golden clusters.

Even though it was raining, she decided to call from where she was – she didn't want to risk calling them from Orchard End. What would Zain and Em think if they saw the salad leaves on the walls? Or overheard her mum going on about how she thought they should have a compost loo?

She thought of Zainab's home: clean white walls, glossy kitchen, shop-bought cordials and snacks in the cupboards. And of the flat Emilia lived in, which was lovely and slightly messy in a relaxing way, with that super-sized tub of hot chocolate that Em always got out.

She took a deep breath of fresh, damp air. *OK. Just do it*, she told herself. *They might not even be around. They're probably having tea . . .*

Zainab and Emilia both answered straight away.

Emilia was in her kitchen. She'd squeezed herself

into a tiny space on the worktop and she had a lollipop in her mouth. Zainab was in her bedroom – clean and tidy with organized shelves – and in front of the laptop. 'What did Charley say?' she asked.

Laurie's mouth went dry. It wasn't as though she'd done anything wrong. And Emilia and Zainab weren't the sort of people to get angry. Why was she so nervous?

'Hang on. Where's Em gone?'

Emilia had disappeared for a sec but reappeared with a jar of pasta sauce. Her mum was working late so she was making herself some dinner.

'Come on then!' said Emilia. 'Spill!'

Laurie said, as lightly as she could, 'I know it sounds weird, but she'd heard of Beauty in the Kitchen and she wants me to work with her for the competition . . .'

Zainab's eyebrows shot up so high you could see them above her glasses. 'What?'

'Whoa!' said Emilia. 'That's incredible! Charley Keating-Sloss! I mean, whoa!'

'Really? You think so?' said Laurie.

'You did say no, didn't you?' Zainab's face came right up close to the screen.

There was a pause.

Emilia smiled. 'It's OK, Laurie.'

'Is it? Laurie on a different team from us just seems so wrong!' Zainab frowned.

'It's only this time!' said Laurie, feeling flustered. Did Zainab have to be so full-on? 'Obviously, I would prefer to work with you.'

'Why did you say yes, then?' Zainab pushed.

Laurie hated that straight-out question. What was she meant to say? That working with Charley gave her a better chance of winning? That would be horrible!

'It's hard to say no to someone like Charley.' She looked at the tiny ferns at her feet and wished she could curl up like they do in the rain and hide away.

'Understood!' said Emilia. She moved the lollipop from one side of her mouth to the other.

Zainab said, 'But we always do really well when we team up. I mean, remember all of those outstanding points we were given when we did that presentation in Science . . . ?'

'It's only a competition!' said Laurie, as lightly as she could. She put her phone-free hand up and nervously pulled at a catkin.

'But this is the biggest thing we've ever entered,' said Zainab.

'And whoever wins will be the most popular person at school,' added Emilia, 'because their class gets to go on a day trip and we get the 4D printer! Do you know you can actually print out chocolates in whatever shape you like on those things? Though to be fair, Charley Keating-Sloss is already popular.'

Zainab huffed. 'Popular? She's not even nice, Em.'

Emilia tipped her head from side to side. 'She can be,' she said, after a moment. 'Remember when she helped raise funds for the hedgehog sanctuary, and she did that assembly on it?'

'Hmm,' sniffed Zainab disapprovingly.

Laurie remembered how the school magazine had

run an article, 'Charley's Charity Chums', about her support of hedgehogs. And how Charley had turned the article into being about her new hairstyle ('Spiked to one side, like my little friends!') and didn't say anything about the plight of the hedgehogs.

'That's the thing about the so-called popular girls,' said Zainab. 'People want to be liked by them or look like them, but no one actually *likes* them.'

'Got to go,' said Emilia. 'My spaghetti's ready. It's all fine, Laurie, if that's what you want. And Zainab, we can have a meeting tomorrow to talk about our entry.'

'OK,' said Zainab with a sigh. 'Maybe this will work. Being in a team of two might make us more focused . . .'

Laurie felt a twinge of annoyance. Zainab was right, she thought. They had always worked in a team of three. But since when hadn't they been focused?

Emilia disappeared from the screen. Quickly, because she felt confused and nervous, Laurie said bye too and clicked off.

CHAPTER EIGHT

> **@StyleFile** My long-time dream has been to launch my own skincare range, with products that are better and sparklier than anything that's out there. And now I've teamed up with **@BeautyintheKitchen** and it's become a thing. YAY! I'M SO excited!!!!!

A couple of days later and the reality of working with Charley had really begun to kick in. Word had got around school faster than you could hit a SHARE button. The effect had been instant, and to Laurie it was like she had become visible for the first time in her life. Suddenly everyone knew her name.

Girls were stopping her in the corridors, messaging her on her School Stories account, and she was late for practically every lesson as she struggled to answer a zillion questions every time she went to get something out of the lockers. Was she going to sell a blueberry body yogurt, like they'd seen on her Beauty in the Kitchen account last month? What about the cacao eye shadow? And what was Charley wearing on her cheeks? She had a really peachy glow – was it something in Laurie's range?

By the Wednesday of the first week of the competition, they were only really meant to have decided on a name for their business, but Charley said they needed to get ahead and have some products ready to sell. That made sense to Laurie, because showing people the products would feel easier than answering questions about them.

She was thinking about what to make while she was walking back from the bus stop, on her way home from school. She stopped for a moment as a pair of pheasants crossed the lane in front of her. The male was a showy display of red, chestnut and gleaming emerald and the female was a subtle speckled cinnamon. Laurie kept watch, in case there was a car coming, so she could keep the birds safe. Her phone buzzed, and she pulled it out of her pocket as the pheasants hopped through the hedgerow and into the fields.

Laurie swiped her screen; it was a message from Charley.

> **@StyleFile** Meet me in the cafe after school tomorrow, and bring a face pack or moisturizer that's got serious cult product potential.

Laurie wasn't exactly sure what 'serious cult product potential' meant. But one idea did flash into Laurie's mind and that was Skin Whisperer, the tomato face serum that she and Fern had once made.

Its major plus points were:

1. It brightened your skin
2. It had unbeatable pick-me-up properties.
3. They had loads of tomatoes at home.

But would Charley regard the Skin Whisperer as a bit of a boring product? At its heart, it was only a plain tomato-based serum that you washed off. It wasn't a sparkly lip gloss or an intoxicatingly chocolate body balm . . .

She decided to go for it. It was a super-quick fix – tomatoes, cornflour and olive oil – and an affordable skin lifesaver. And it really did give your skin a glow. As she walked, Laurie flicked back on to School Stories. There was a new video from Amy, one of the celebrity judges for The Disruptors. She clicked PLAY.

The scene was a busy, crowded shopping centre. There was a loud beating soundtrack and a shot of Amy's blue and orange trainers. Then Amy stopped and stared straight at the camera, pointed her finger and said, 'You're here to be the silver lining in this tough economy. To prove that even though you're young, even though times are hard –' the camera showed boarded-up shops – 'YOU have the spark to still make millions.' Amy spun around in the street, and the video faded out.

Millions! Laurie ran her hand along the tips of the spiky hedgerow and a shower of white petals flew off the hawthorn blossom. *What would I buy first*, she thought, *if I had millions?* First she'd buy hot chocolate at the cafe and then she'd book a holiday abroad! She smiled to herself, imagining her parents, Fern and Radzi playing on a beach, with white sands, rolling seas and lots of ice cream.

But then Laurie's chest tightened. She loved their camping holidays in Cornwall and she understood why her parents couldn't justify flying because of the climate crisis. She'd never want her mum and dad to believe that she thought going abroad was better than Cornwall, because it wasn't. But it was hard when people at school went to far-flung places.

The next time Emilia jetted off to see her relatives in Poland, or Zainab mentioned how she was going to Italy with her mum and her brother, Laurie really wanted to be able to say that she and Fern were going somewhere popular and abroad. *Ooh, we could get a train to France,* she thought. *Mum and Dad might like that . . .*

Laurie looked at her screen. Another clip had started playing. There was a close-up of Avril's trainers, which were covered in rainbow sequins.

She was tapping her feet. 'Anyone can have amazing ideas. The difference is that entrepreneurs make their ideas happen. Engage! Inspire! Influence!' Avril eyeballed the camera. 'Sometimes the only way to demonstrate your commitment to one thing is by saying no to another.'

Laurie was at the very end of the lane now. On one side there were fields, with cows and sheep, and on the other there was a stream gently winding its way around an apple orchard. The water drifted past Orchard End.

Laurie put her key into the front door. She needed to get going on the Skin Whisperer straight away. She needed to make her ideas happen.

She stepped into the hallway: wafts of garlic, ginger and soy sauce hit Laurie in the face. The smell was unmistakeable. Eau de Dad's Cooking.

'That you, Lau?' came her dad's voice from the kitchen.

'Glad you're back! Would you mind grabbing some lime leaves?'

'Sure.' Laurie pulled off a couple from the tree beside the stairs.

'We're having crispy tofu noodles.'

Perfect. She'd have dinner and then get going on the Skin Whisperer straight away.

It was less than three weeks until the competition was over. Which meant she only needed to stay engaged, inspired and influential for nineteen days: 456 hours. She smiled. How hard could it be?

Somehow, though, finding the time that evening was near-on impossible.

For a start, Radzi was causing chaos in the kitchen. He was test-piloting the latest virtual reality headset. It was sleek and thin – a bit like Radzi – and the game he was playing seemed to have convinced him he was deep in the rainforest, catching silver beetles.

He was smacking his hands together at what looked

like thin air and getting in everyone's way.

'Gotcha!' he yelled, slapping the air above Laurie's head.

Laurie ducked out of Radzi's way and went to shake the wok of noodles, while her dad went to the pantry to get his home-made tofu.

Her mum was sitting at the piano, on the far side of the kitchen, talking about her day at work. She ran Cook & Book events – she went into libraries and community centres and made food with people, based on their favourite stories.

Today, though, she'd introduced a bunch of pre-schoolers to the joys of garbage guzzling. As ever, her mum was setting her anecdote to music by banging out notes to create tension. Laurie found it annoying.

'We were making a plant-based snake crumble from *The Gruffalo*,' said her mum. She thumped the piano. 'We used mushrooms for the snake, by the way. And I looked out of the window and I saw a guy throwing out red peppers, near the back doors of the market –' she hit some high, fluttery notes – 'like that! And I thought, red peppers?'

'Come back here!' interrupted Radzi, shaking his fists.

'So we ran out – had to take the kids with me, obviously – our hands covered in flour . . .' Her mum banged on the pedals for added drama.

'Can you add the spring onions, Lau?' Dad shouted. 'Should be on the side.'

Laurie was only half listening as she stirred the noodles, giving the occasional murmur of interest in response to what her mum was saying ('Amazing what happens when you pretend red peppers are snakes' tongues!').

The rest of Laurie's thoughts were taken up with Skin Whisperer and the packaging she needed for it. She was wondering if they had any empty, biodegradable yogurt pots when Fern came crashing into the kitchen.

'Laurie!' Fern's hair was billowing behind her. 'We're going out flyering after tea!'

'What?'

'We've got to tell people about the free food we're taking to March for Climate.' Fern squeezed Laurie's arm. 'We made flyers and we're going to drop them through doors!'

OK, Laurie thought, *this is a test, isn't it?* Avril had said on that video that the way to demonstrate your commitment was by saying no to something else. She bit her lip. And Fern's flyering was the something else.

Her mum was nodding. 'We thought the leaflets would start a conversation, and we can build on that by talking to people during the march.'

Her dad dished up the noodles. 'Plan is to eat this before we go – and that when we get back.' He tipped his head towards the plum cobbler on the worktop.

'Can we have pudding first?' said Fern. She stared at the deep scone topping, with the sweet plum juice oozing around the sides. 'Looks way nicer.'

'No.' Laurie's dad handed her a bowl of noodles. 'Leafleting – or flyering, as you like to call it – is hard work.' His eyes were shining, as if he couldn't wait to get started. 'We'll need it when we get home.'

'Lau, poke Radzi, would you?' said her mum. She was now putting forks and glasses of water on the table. 'Tell him tea's ready.'

'Dig in, everyone,' said Laurie's dad once they were all seated.

'SorrybutIcan'tcome,' Laurie mumbled.

'What?' asked her dad.

'I'm busy tonight.' Laurie put her hand on Fern's arm. 'Sorry, Ferny, but—'

'What?' Fern looked shocked.

'Thought you did your homework before breakfast?' said her mum.

Laurie felt her chest flutter. 'It's not that. I've got to make some beauty products for—'

'Don't tell me!' Fern cut in. 'The competition.'

Laurie's cheeks went hot. 'You said you didn't mind me selling the Beauty in the Kitchen stuff! That you wanted people to see how good our recipes are!'

'I don't mind about you using the recipes,' said Fern.

She pulled a sorrowful puppy look. 'It's just that I never see you any more.'

'Aah,' said Laurie's mum.

'That's ridiculous!' said Laurie. 'Why are you sticking up for her? The competition was only announced two days ago. What time have we lost, Fern?'

Laurie's dad put his fork down 'Lau, you did say it wouldn't interfere with you helping to highlight food waste.'

'It'll only take an hour,' her mum said briskly.

'An hour!' She wouldn't even be able to start on the products until after eight o'clock.

Her dad finished a mouthful of tofu. 'Your extra pair of hands really will make a difference. Never forget the family motto.' He pointed to the postcard on the fridge of the three Cs, which the Larksies had long ago adopted as their road map for life.

Connection. Compassion. Contribution.

Laurie rolled her eyes. She knew the three Cs were important, and of course she tried to live by those values. *But come on!* She felt a fierce spark of frustration. She could think of some Cs she wished her family had more of. Cash, for a start. Chocolate. And . . . She needed a word for being more mainstream, more average. Conventional! What would happen if she put *those* words on the fridge?

'And please come, Laurie,' said Fern, 'because if you ask me—'

'Nobody did ask you,' Laurie cut in, her voice breaking a little.

'It's compassion too!'

Laurie felt like throwing her noodles at her. *I'll give you compassion, Fern! I'm on a crazy tight deadline to make some beauty products. For a massive competition! So, how about some* compassion *for me?*

'Well, it is compassion!' said Fern furiously. 'Because if some people are throwing away food and others don't have enough, then that's totally unfair! And what about the energy that's wasted from growing the food that's chucked! Anyone with compassion should—'

'It's not that I don't have *compassion*,' Laurie interrupted, equally hotly. 'Of course I care about people going hungry! It's that I don't have TIME.'

Laurie looked at Radzi. During family disputes, he was as silent as the gooseberries on the bush behind the table. Laurie speared a piece of red pepper and shoved it into her mouth. He must see how unfair they were being. She wished that he would stick up for her.

Fern started angling her face at Laurie. 'Purlease . . .'

'You know we wouldn't ask you to do this unless we felt it was important,' said Laurie's mum at last. 'It's not as if you've got homework.'

'Yes, but—'

Her dad looked serious. 'We feel you've done enough on the competition for this week. Every time I look at you, you've got your face down on your phone!'

'But—'

'You know what? No buts,' said Mum sharply. 'This is an opportunity for some fresh air and to be together as a family.'

Laurie slumped down on her chair. Talk about unfair. She knew that she'd said she would help out with the march, but that didn't mean that she had the time to push leaflets through doors.

She heaved herself up, cleared the last few plates from the table and went into the hallway. Her dad pulled his coat down from the pegs.

Not the coat, thought Laurie, her heart sinking.

It was an orange puffer jacket. The sort that some boys in Laurie's class wore and the sort that no other dad would ever wear in a million years. In fact, no one who wasn't at school should have one. There should be a legal maximum age, printed on the label of garments like that: *Over 18s prohibited.*

'Don't start!' said Laurie's dad, pointing at her. He laughed and zipped it right up to the collar. 'I thought you said this was the height of fashion?'

'If you're twelve, Dad!'

Laurie felt annoyance rise up in her. Just because Tom, her dad's friend, had given him that coat – apparently,

Tom's son had grown out of it and they'd given it to her dad because he'd always said he liked it – didn't mean he had to wear it.

'I mean, it was kind of Tom and everything,' said Laurie. 'But . . .'

'It's warm!' Her dad patted the duvet-like material. 'And it's very practical for when I'm standing on the picket lines at work.'

'Even I can't believe you wear that thing,' said Fern. 'That orange is so bright! You'd look better in a coat of another colour, like maybe black?'

Laurie's mum came into the hallway. 'Oranges are not the only coats!' She laughed, as if she'd cracked a joke.

'Any more from the Fashion Police,' said her dad, 'and I'm going to tuck my jeans into my socks. And put my hood up . . .'

Laurie rolled her eyes. 'Let's go.'

What happened to demonstrating her commitment to one thing by saying no to another?

*

The evening was warm and breezy, blossom was swirling from the trees like confetti. And Fern had this quality – their mum called it a survival mechanism – that meant even though she was capable of really winding people up, the next second she would be so incredibly sweet and funny that no one ever stayed mad at her for long.

As they walked, Fern was reading aloud from a book that their dad had written called *On the Doorstep of Your Mind*. He had written it about his years on the campaign trail, for everything from General Elections to stopping fast food outlets from opening near schools. Fern was reading out things like, *'Smile. Even when people argue with everything you say, or are rude, or slam the door in your face, always smile. That way, even if they don't remember anything you said about the campaign, at least they'll remember that you were friendly!'*

Laurie's dad was laughing and saying what good advice it was. And her mum was going on about the march and how they needed to get across the message that although there was no stigma to eating surplus food, the food industry shouldn't be creating it in the first place.

Laurie stayed silent. She felt too tired to get into another argument. She did roll her eyes once or twice though, and genuinely wondered whether her mum had ever been to high school. She would like to see her mum going to her school and saying her lunch came from the bins. *No stigma? As if!*

The leaflets themselves were really nice – Fern had illustrated them with cakes, fruit and sandwiches – so Laurie didn't mind putting them through doors. Laurie and her mum did one side of the road, and Fern and her dad did the other.

But it was hard to relax when her phone started buzzing with messages from Charley. She was doing her usual stuff – posting inspirational photos of her vast shoe collection – but Laurie's heart started to beat faster when she read a post about the competition:

Words like 'standout' and 'cult product' obviously got people excited, because the messages were getting lots of likes. But to Laurie, who didn't even have anything to sell right now, it felt like a shovel-load of pressure. And when they finally got home, things got worse because Laurie's mum told her she looked exhausted and insisted that she went straight to bed.

There was no point arguing when her mum got like that, so Laurie ate her pudding on the bottom bunk with Fern. Her plan was to get up afterwards – she'd look sparkier and less tired after the pudding, so it would be easier to convince her mum that she was perfectly able to whip up a load of products with serious cult potential.

But Laurie's eyes were drooping, and as soon as she put down her spoon she felt utterly exhausted. She told herself that she'd just close her eyes for a minute, but she was soon fast asleep. Which meant by the time she woke up she still hadn't made a single product.

Go, go, GO! Laurie clattered down the stairs the next morning. There was still time to make the Skin Whisperer.

But she'd have to hurry . It was already eight o'clock.

As Laurie ran into the kitchen, she was trying really hard to stay upbeat and positive. She was even thinking that she and Charley could do a vlog at breaktime to promote the product. It could start with Charley looking a bit washed out. She paused. *LOL! When had Charley ever looked less than radiant?*

Laurie opened the fridge, feeling very thankful that Skin Whisperer was so easy to make and needed only a few basic ingredients.

But as she assessed the contents of the fridge she felt a fizz of panic. *Where were the tomatoes?* Tomatoes were essential to Whisperer. They were laden with antioxidants and rich in skin-brightening vitamin C, which was partly why the product worked so well.

And they had piles of them! Laurie and Fern had laughed about how there were enough to start a food-fight festival like La Tomatina when their mum had brought home those boxes.

Laurie raced frantically around the kitchen and checked everywhere, from the fruit basket on the window sill to the fridge. Nada. Nothing. Not a tomato in sight.

Panicking, she shouted, 'Where are the tomatoes?'

'On the hallway ceiling?' Her mum called down from upstairs.

'Not those! Most of those are still green at the moment! I meant those squashy ones from the market.'

Her mum didn't reply. Laurie could hear the hairdryer so there was no point shouting again.

Where were the others? She opened the front door. Radzi was doing yoga beside the magnolia tree – with a virtual headset on, making him believe he was on a white sandy beach in the Hebrides. Her dad was outside on the driveway, getting ready for work, and she guessed Fern was still in bed.

Laurie ran outside. Her dad ran a trade union for gig-economy workers, and this morning he was attaching a banner that read *Workplaces not Workhouses!* to his bike.

'Where are the tomatoes?'

'When life gives you tomatoes . . .' her dad replied, grinning.

'What?'

'Radzi made tomato ketchup! Remember?'

Laurie's eyes went wide. *How could she have forgotten?* The other day, Radzi had turned the kitchen into a steamy witches' cavern, chopping, simmering, sieving and blending tomatoes into a thick, rich, spicy sauce. They'd had it on tarragon and bean sausages, and with millet burgers, and it had been great, and everything. Only now . . .

Laurie sprinted back inside and opened the pantry. The shelves were stacked with jars and bottles of Radzi's ketchup and it made her want to scream.

'What's he doing? Stockpiling them in case of a nuclear war?'

'Don't joke about things like that, Lau,' said her dad solemnly as he walked into the kitchen. He popped his head around the door. 'But while you're there, pass me a jar, would you? I'm going to be on the picket line with some delivery drivers today. There's a place that kindly gives us some free burgers, but I'll be honest, they aren't up to much.'

Laurie mutely gave one to her dad.

He put it his pocket. 'Thanks. This will improve the offering no end. What did you say you needed tomatoes for?'

'To hydrate, exfoliate,' said Laurie sharply, 'and restore radiance with a simple, ultra-effective, face serum.'

'Right you are,' he replied. 'How about we get the stepladders out later and pick some from the ceiling. Give them a day or two to ripen?'

'Thanks, Dad,' said Laurie quietly. 'But the thing is, I need them now.'

Laurie was getting more and more worried. It felt like her anxious thoughts were releasing themselves into the air like the noxious mould spores on gone-off food, and multiplying like mad.

Her mum came down the stairs, hair blow-dried and flicked-up at the ends.

'Why do people have to use the last of everything?' muttered Laurie to herself. She picked a handful of spelt flakes from the jar and put them in her mouth.

'Don't do that,' said Laurie's mum automatically. 'Pour yourself a bowl.' She looked at the oven clock. 'Gosh, don't want to panic you, Lau, but it's twenty-five past.'

'Twenty-five past?' *Now I'm really up against it*, Laurie thought, her chest swirling with worry.

OK. She had to not freak out.

The recipe called for a tomato to be scored (an X through the base, with a sharp knife) and plunged into boiling water. So that was basically cooked tomato, wasn't it? And what's ketchup, at the end of the day? Cooked tomato!

'For breakfast,' her mum was saying, 'I can stick some

toast on but you'd have to eat it on the bus. Or there's molasses flapjack?'

But Laurie had more urgent things to worry about than breakfast.

Her heart pounding, she chucked a load of ketchup into a bowl and threw in the oil and cornflour. She gave it a mix, poured it into biodegradable pots, grabbed a flapjack and raced out of the door.

CHAPTER NINE

'Pick a word that describes you,' said Laurie. She lent on the desk in the school library at lunchtime and read a list out to Emilia and Zainab. '(a) funny, (b) romantic, or (c) brave.'

She looked at Emilia, who was staring at her piece of paper blankly.

'Wake up! We're doing the perfume quiz, remember? So I can work out which scents might sell best for the competition.'

Emilia looked dreamy. 'Sorry. But funny, romantic . . . brave? It was like you were describing Ben Kalu there!' Laurie suppressed an eye roll. Ben Kalu was a Year Niner. He was tall, with heartstopper eyes and a knockout sense of style.

'Well, I suppose he's brave to wear that cardigan,' teased Zainab.

Emilia laughed. 'Very funny, Zain. I need a scent to attract Ben, don't I?' She pulled her knees up on the seat. 'What smells completely irresistible?'

'Treacle tart?' said Laurie.

'Agreed! That's your scent idea sorted, then.'

Zainab folded her arms and smiled. 'But back to talking of crushes. You never mention anyone, Laurie! You have to tell us who you like. Otherwise we're going to have to assume it's Elliot. You two are so competitive in assessments!'

'He just likes beating me, for some reason. It doesn't mean we're in love!'

Laurie went red. *Why did I say the word 'love'?*

'Love?' shrieked Emilia. 'I hadn't realized it was *that* serious.' She put her arms up. 'Hey, don't do your cross face! I'm only joking.'

'I know, sorry.'

It seemed essential to have a crush at Silverdale – yet another thing to be worried about. It needed to be someone that no one else was interested in –

she couldn't go for Ben Kalu or Zainab's crush Daniel Sydnom, obviously, because she would never do that to her friends. But for now, she needed to change the subject.

'Love the hair, by the way,' said Laurie. She gently lifted a strand of Emilia's hair, which Emilia had paid to be sprayed neon pink by a team called 'Do or Dye' in Year 8, before school that day.

'I'd get mine done but my hair is so dark –' Zainab picked up a strand of glossy, slick-straight hair – 'that the pink wouldn't show up.'

'Same,' said Laurie. 'By the way, though, Zain, I've got a new recipe for a beetroot conditioner that should work on your hair.'

'Yes please!' said Zainab.

'It looks like pink custard but it made my hair feel great.'

'And in exchange, you can have one of our doggy birthday bags,' said Zainab.

She and Emilia had decided to make home-made

dog biscuits, from grated carrot and oats, and sell them in birthday bags, with ribbons and gift tags. It was working well because Zainab's mum had put some on the reception desk at the veterinary clinic where she worked.

'I know you don't have a dog but they make great presents for any pooch in your life,' said Emilia.

'Which is basically your dog,' said Laurie, 'as Bella is the dog I see most often!'

'Well, Bella would love you for it,' said Emilia.

'Sorted! Back to it. Are you (a) an optimist, (b) a pessimist, or (c) a realist?'

'Realist,' said Zainab.

'Optimist,' said Emilia.

Laurie scrolled down the 'What's Your Signature Scent?' quiz she'd written. She'd made it up ages ago, based on research she'd done online, and thought it would come in handy now she needed to make some perfume.

'Which word describes you best: (a) helpful, (b) powerful, or (c) resourceful?'

'Resourceful?' said Zainab immediately. 'I managed to make some splints out of lollipop sticks when our hamster broke her leg and my mum was still out at work.'

'That's cool!'

'Helpful, because we're doing this quiz for you,' said Emilia.

'Do you like eating (a) crisp red apples, (b) a crispbread, or (c) actual crisps?'

'Easy,' said Emilia, writing down her answer. 'I love apples.'

'And I love crisps,' said Zainab.

'Would you rather (a) climb a mountain, (b) trek through a forest, or (c) swim the English Channel?'

'Getting my swimming costume now,' said Zainab.

Laurie checked the time – lunch break was nearly over, which meant they had Spanish class next, then ITC, and then it was time to meet Charley at the cafe. She gulped. Swimming the Channel felt like an easier option.

'OK, nearly done. If you were a pizza topping . . .'

'I think I'd quite like to be,' said Emilia, leaning her head down on the desk.

'. . . would you be (a) pineapple, (b) cheese and tomato, or (c) sausage?'

'Impossible!' said Emilia. 'I love pineapple *and* sausage!'

'You'd have liked the pizzas that Fern and I did for the RR—'

'The what?' said Zainab.

'Nothing,' said Laurie, her cheeks flushing.

After a couple more questions, Laurie added up the scores.

'OK, you were mainly As,' she said to Emilia. 'So, your signature scent is an uplifting, happy-go-lucky, exotic mix. You suit notes of lime, coconut and maybe cardamom and geranium.'

'Sounds delish!'

'And Zain, you were mostly Cs, so you need aquatic notes, with sparkling citrus top notes, like lemon or lime, and a thoughtful oil, like basil.'

'Like it,' said Zainab.

'That's given me some great ideas, thanks. I'll make some perfumes tonight. And I'll give you free bottles, of course!'

'Thanks,' said Zainab. 'But you don't have to. We can buy some!'

'No, you're welcome,' said Laurie. 'You've helped with this.'

'What about you?' said Emilia. 'You should do this on yourself!'

Laurie had, countless times. And every time the answer was the same. According to the quiz, Laurie was as sweet, warm and comforting as vanilla. But she could hardly tell them that, because for some reason, people seemed to think that vanilla was really plain and boring. Laurie absolutely *loved* vanilla. To her, it was long summers in the garden, eating the creamiest, smoothest ice cream in the world, as well as cosy winter evenings with Fern having crumble and custard together beside the fire, in their pyjamas. But she needed her signature scent to say 'elegant, dynamic, sophisticated', not 'sponge cake'.

'Great idea,' she said.

Charley was at the cafe before Laurie. And the reason Laurie knew this was because of all the photos Charley was posting on School Stories. The barista had squiggled a heart in cocoa powder on the froth and Charley had written:

> **@StyleFile** Strong, creamy, utterly addictive. Heart-thumping good . . . #HotChocolate! #ThursdayTreats.

She'd photographed the drink on one of the handmade wooden tables, so you could see the backdrop of the cafe. There were the old-fashioned treacle tins filled with sugar, marshmallow-pink cushions and a stack of cinnamon pastries.

When Laurie entered, Charley immediately shouted, 'Here!' and beckoned Laurie over, like she was a waitress.

She gestured at the chair opposite.

'You know Elise and Orla?'

Laurie tried to smile, but her throat felt constricted. Elise and Orla were Charley's best friends and featured regularly in her feed. *'I have a girl gang that is deeply enviable,'* Charley had written on a recent StyleFile post. There was an image of the three of them, in different coloured T-shirts (by the same fashion brand). *'My friends are some of the most uplifting people that anyone could ever meet. Their radiance leaves me feeling brighter, more inspired and more truly myself.'* Charley hadn't told Laurie that they would be there.

'Well, I recognize them from your posts on StyleFile.'

She had been nervous enough meeting up with Charley, but if she'd known the deeply enviable girl gang was going to be here, she wasn't sure she would have had the courage to come. In fact, she knew she wouldn't.

Charley looked excited. 'They've agreed to be our future taste-makers.'

'Our what?'

'Influencers, trendsetters, brand ambassadors, whatever!' Charley said, expanding her arms. 'I've signed them up. Isn't that amazing?'

Elise giggled. 'You are pretty persuasive.'

Charley continued. 'The idea is that you give them some products and they'll showcase them at school. Think about it. Is there any better way to promote our products than having them recommended by social connectors like Elise and Orla?'

'Social connectors?'

'They've both got real-life influence at school as well as on social media.'

Laurie looked unconvinced.

'Not as much as me? I know!' Charley said with a laugh. 'Don't worry. I'll be the main face behind the products. Having Elise and Orla do it too will just amplify our marketing.'

Orla nodded. 'We'll stay on core message.' Her ponytail was bobbing up and down. It was identical to Elise's side pony, only Elise wore hers on the left and Orla on the right. Charley's was high and central. Laurie wondered whether they messaged each other every morning, to check they were wearing them in the right place.

'Because we want to support Char,' said Elise, in a sing-song babyish voice. She touched Charley's arm.

'Expect some gorgeous free products,' said Charley, looking at her friends. 'And you, Laurie, can expect lots of glowy looks. So, come on, let's see what you've got.'

Laurie pulled her bag on to her lap. The others were going on about the flashy celebrity-inspired cosmetics that their mothers and sisters wore. *Thank goodness they can't see my mum's dressing table*, thought Laurie.

She took a deep breath. 'Meet your new cosmetic warrior.'

Charley, Orla and Elise exchanged excited looks.

'This is Skin Whisperer.' Laurie handed them each a pot. She put the rest on the table. 'A supercharged serum that's ultra-simple, uber-effective.'

Elise's face dropped. 'OMG, that looks way weird.'

Don't panic, Laurie told herself. *It looks fine.* Some of the cornflour had clumped together and the oil was sitting on the top. It looked like someone had thrown lumps of flour into greasy tomato ketchup. Laurie grabbed a wooden stirrer from the cafe table and gave one of the pots a good mix, until the serum was pink and smooth. She forced herself to sound breezy. 'It's got the astringent elements of tomatoes . . .'

Orla leaned forward. 'Tomatoes are so in right now.'

'And the soothing quality of olive oil.'

Elise's nose wrinkled. 'The smell reminds me of something.'

Laurie waved the bottle across her face as if it were magic. 'It makes your skin look like it's wearing an Instagram filter.'

Elise and Orla visibly perked up.

Laurie handed a bottle to Charley.

Charley sniffed it and gave a doubtful look.

Then she grinned at the others. 'One, two, three!' She took the wooden stirrer from Laurie and used it to dot and dab the serum on her face. 'Awesome! I can feel it working already . . . Here comes a super-smooth complexion.'

Charley then took a selfie at a flatteringly high, overhead angle. Her thumbs flew over her screen writing a caption and she posted it straight to School Stories.

Instantly everyone's alerts went off. Laurie checked her phone. Charley had filtered the photo with a warm wash of colour, with golden highlights that made her cheeks shine.

> **@StyleFile** An au naturel skin serum exists NOW that literally transforms your face. You Need It #DFTBA.

Immediately people were approaching their table.

'Look!' said a girl. Laurie recognized her. Rizwana was the Lower School hockey captain. She was often pictured in the school magazine, with the team around her, holding up a cup. 'There she is now!'

Charley sat up, her face dotted with ketchup. Before Rizwana had even got there, another voice shouted out: 'Charley K-S!' Another Year 9 girl called Sophie was racing over.

'We saw your post about the skin serum,' said Rizwana.

'Looks amazing,' said Sophie.

Rizwana laughed. 'And then we turned around, and there you were!'

'Are you wearing it now?' Sophie said breathlessly.

'Certainly am.'

Charley pulled a strand of hair away from where it was sticking to the gloop. She threw a discreet, slightly disgusted look at Laurie and spoke so quietly, it was barely audible in Laurie's ear. 'Looks like the sludge in the school canteen food waste container.'

Laurie nearly dropped the yogurt pot. 'I made it fresh this morning, from ingredients in my kitchen!'

Charley lowered her voice even more. 'Yes, but remember, I know where your family goes shopping! Beauty in the Kitchen? Beauty from the bottom of the bin, more like!'

Laurie's stomach was whizzing so fast it felt like someone had stuck it in a food processor. 'How can you say that?' she gasped.

Charley did her tinkly laugh. She waved her hand at Laurie as if nothing had happened. Then she turned back to the girls, who were excitedly chatting about the new product, with an angelic smile on her face.

'Listen up, people! This is a skin warrior.'

'Whisperer,' said Laurie, automatically. 'It's the Skin Whisperer.'

'Warrior!' said Charley, firmly. She threw her arms out into some kind of Boudica pose. 'So get ready to meet your face's new BFF.'

Wow, thought Laurie. Charley was gleaming and confident, and it was hard not to admire the way that she could speak in front of people. From the upbeat, positive way she was introducing the serum, no one would know she'd just been really rude to the person who'd made it, although Laurie noticed that Charley was starting to shoot her some funny looks, and was touching her face a bit too often.

'Ooh, where do you get it?' said Sophie.

'Have you got some here?' Rizwana looked keen.

Charley handed out the pots on the table.

'Please can I take one for my sister too?' said Sophie.

Laurie's hands were shaking as she gave her another pot.

Other girls had appeared by then, who it turned out also knew Charley. There was lots of excited chatter and shouts of 'Us too, please!'

Charley said, 'I've got a couple more pots here, as it happens.'

Orla's mouth dropped open. 'I thought we were, like, the—'

'Brand influ—' said Elise, looking shocked.

Charley flashed them a look.

They handed the pots over.

'Looks good,' Rizwana said. 'I'm sick of the wind chill when I'm playing hockey. I need something protective on my face.'

Sophie smiled. 'If my skin ends up looking anything like as good as yours, Charley, I'll be a customer for life.'

They all laughed.

Everyone was dipping their fingers into the pots and applying the serum to their faces.

'Ooh, it's rather stingy, actually,' said Rizwana, after a moment. She had her hand to her cheek and her eyes were watering.

'It's packed with active ingredients,' said Charley smoothly. 'So that's a sign the serum is working.' She stared hard at Laurie. 'What's in it again?'

Laurie hesitated.

'Tomatoes?' prompted Charley.

'And olive oil,' said Laurie.

'Which is very soothing,' Charley said in her clipped tones.

'Fresh herbs.'

That was true, wasn't it? She was sure Radzi had thrown some basil in from the walls when he was making the ketchup to give it more flavour, along with his trademark kick of chilli.

Oh. My . . .

Chilli!

Laurie's heart suddenly felt like it was on fire. The tomato ketchup had CHILLI in it. It must have. Radzi put it on absolutely everything. He practically sprinkled it on his breakfast cereal. With horrible clarity Laurie realized why Rizwana's face was stinging. And if her cheeks were tingling, then Charley's – who had had it on for much longer – must be absolutely burning up.

Don't panic, Laurie told herself. *Stay calm*. She stared at the floor and tried to think of anything she'd ever read or been told about chilli. It couldn't kill you or anything – everyone would know. It would be on safety notices, like the ones that say you can't drink bleach. There'd have to be a symbol, a skull and crossbones. Or a massive DANGER sign on spicy foods. *May Contain Chilli*. *There would*, thought Laurie desperately, *wouldn't there*?

'What's up?' said Charley sharply.

'Time for those face masks to come off,' said Laurie, trying to make her voice sound casual. 'Go, go, go! It only takes a second to work!'

The whole lot of them disappeared into the loos,

leaving Laurie beside the bags. The second the bathroom door swung shut, she grabbed her phone and did a search for 'Can you put fresh chilli on your face?'

She fell back on the sofa, relief cooling her insides. It wasn't exactly a recommended practice. But neither was it life threatening. In fact, further down the pages, she found a beauty vlogger who had a recipe for chilli face masks.

Apparently, the anti-inflammatory properties of peppers can help tackle acne and stimulate blood flow. The vlogger's complexion looked amazing. Though that could have been the filter.

In any case, chilli cheeks or not, there was a noticeable upswing in energy around Charley as she and her entourage emerged from the bathroom. She told Laurie that already they'd received thirteen orders.

Sophie had her wallet out. 'How much?'

'Seeing as it's you,' said Charley. She touched Sophie and Rizwana lightly on each of their shoulders. 'Three pounds. That's a special introductory price. Orders we've already had qualify for that offer, after that it's a fiver a go.'

Five pounds! Was Charley joking? You wouldn't pay that for a full-price bottle of ketchup, let alone one diluted with oil, water and cornflour. There's no way Laurie's friends could pay that much. She'd have to talk to Charley about charging less to Year 7s . . .

Everyone was heading back to their tables or leaving the cafe, grinning like they'd scooped the bargain of the year.

Laurie's heart was beating like crazy. 'Remember, this is supercharged serum. Leave it on for sixty seconds max. That's all it needs!'

She gripped the edge of one of the tables to steady her. She tried to imagine how this would look if it was reported on School Stories. *'Someone sold chilli tomato ketchup face sprays for £3. And yes, people bought them.'*

A second later, Charley slapped Laurie on the back. 'Don't look so worried!' She grinned. 'We're going to totally storm this thing.'

CHAPTER TEN

@**TheDisruptors** Countdown! We know it's only week one but it's Friday! A good time to start making some sales! So get out there and promote your product!

When Laurie arrived at the school gates the following day, Emilia nearly knocked her flying.

'Where have you been? I thought we were meeting early? I can't find Zain either.'

No wonder, thought Laurie. The place was packed! She looked around. The school field was usually just a place that everyone scurried through, heads down on their phones, on their way from the bus to the cloakrooms. But today, teams of Disruptors had started going up to people asking if they wanted to buy anything. By the time Laurie arrived, there was a full-on, hectic crowd.

'Want some?' Emilia offered Laurie a bag of spinach pakora. 'Bought this from some Year Eights.' She pointed to three boys, all of whom were called Alex, who were selling the hot snacks. 'Came with a wedge of lemon.' Emilia squeezed on some juice. 'Yum.'

'Dates!' shouted Zoe.

'Only a pound for three!' said Annie, waving the tray around near Laurie. Her mouth watered at the sight of the medjool dates stuffed with tahini and rolled in cacao, decorated with delicate edible flowers.

'They look amazing.'

'Yeah, I've had three.' Emilia slurped her drink. She now had a strawberry smoothie in her hand.

Exactly how much money does Em have? thought Laurie. She tried to fight the feeling of envy. It wasn't that she didn't want Em to have money. She just wanted some too.

But if she asked for money for dates, she knew what would happen. Her mum and dad would dance about the kitchen, saying something like, 'You wanna the dates? We gotta the dates!' And they'd tell her she could help herself to the ones from the fridge.

And that's really nice of them and she didn't want to seem spoiled, but what she really wanted was a *bought* date. With an edible flower. Her chest tightened. Or one of those blueberry muffins. Or a pot of glittery slime.

Anything, really . . .

Laurie could see slices of toast with lovely toppings, personalized stationery, reconditioned headphones, offers of coding lessons, dance workshops, and drone loans. And there was a 'Sunny Snowflakes' scheme. It was about pairing younger pupils with older ones for weekly meet-ups, a sort of mentor/friendship arrangement.

Emilia pointed it out to Laurie. 'This thing is great,' she said. 'You pay a pound but it's a donation really, because they've already pledged to give the money to a mental health charity. I've signed up because I'm hoping –' she dropped her voice to a whisper – 'to be paired with Ben Kalu!'

'Shouldn't work but it does,' sighed Emilia as Ben wandered past. Ben wore this knitted cardigan every single day, instead of the usual fleecy school jumper. On any other boy the look would have been total grandad, but somehow, on Ben that cardigan practically redefined knitwear.

Laurie pulled a face. Ben was rumoured to have a serious crush on Charley. They had been spotted standing next to each other in the lunch queue on several occasions. 'Not sure getting together with Ben is the point of Sunny Snowflakes.'

Laurie looked across the field. Zainab was coming towards them, from the direction of a group of Year 9 girls who were waving PE T-shirts about on sticks. One of them was holding up a sign that read *T-Date or Not to Date?*

'Zainab!' Emilia shouted. 'What's T-Date?'

Zainab came rushing over. She was with Annie and Zoe, who had nearly sold all of their stuffed dates.

'It's nothing like our dates!' said Zoe.

'So it's not a competitor or anything!' Annie said breathlessly. 'We were worried at first, but . . .' She pushed the tray of tahini dates towards Laurie. 'Hey, do you want the last one? Bit bashed but it should taste OK.'

'Thanks!' Laurie ate the date, but she felt bad not paying for it, so she told Annie and Zoe they could have free samples of Skin Warrior.

'You give the T-Dates team your PE T-shirt after you've done PE, and it's all sweaty,' explained Zoe. 'They've got a box, you drop it in, so everything's anonymous . . .'

'Then you sniff all the other T-shirts,' said Annie. 'I know! Sounds disgusting but . . .'

'It's backed up by science.' Zainab sounded earnest. 'You pick out the top that you think smells the best. Or the least offensive . . .'

'And that's your perfect match!' said Annie joyfully.

'It's based on sweat pheromones,' said Zainab. 'Apparently, it's a well-known fact that you're attracted to the sweat of your perfect mate. So, this service helps you find the person you're most compatible with in the whole school.'

'You've done it, haven't you?' said Emilia, grinning. 'I can tell!'

Zainab had so much excitement inside her she looked like she could breathe out bubbles. 'You'll never guess who I got?'

Laurie laughed. 'Well, we can because you're pulling your crushing-on-Daniel-Sydnom face.'

Zainab flushed. 'You got me.'

'But it's PE T-shirts,' said Laurie.

Emilia's eyebrows furrowed. 'So . . . haven't they got name labels in them?'

Just then, the bell rang for morning registration, and they headed into class. As they walked to their form room, Annie explained, 'They only let you see the armpits when you're sniffing.'

Emilia wrinkled her nose. 'Nice!'

'I know, it's complete puke,' said Zoe as they walked past the lockers. 'Nearly heaved. Had to get my orange out of my lunch bag and peel it straight away to get a better smell in my nose.'

Laurie suddenly had a great idea. If people were going to T-Dates and retching because of the smell, maybe she could stand next to them and sell perfume . . . She could mix up some scents to revive people who've breathed in loads of sporty sweat. Watermelon and lime, or rose! Maybe they could collaborate with T-Dates and offer a discount if people bought the dating test and a perfume together?

By lunchtime things had totally kicked off on School Stories, as well as in real life. There was a rumour going around that Skin Warrior was toxic and dangerous. Well, it was less of a rumour and more of a massive shout out on social media as well as up and down the school corridors. The first Laurie heard about it was when her phone buzzed coming out of History:

@StyleFile EXPLAIN!

Charley had forwarded a photo that Sophie had posted of her little sister's face, with her cheeks glowing slightly too much, and the message:

> **@SophieHair** Bought Skin Whisperer? TOSS RIGHT NOW. #toxic #stingingcheeks #ripoff

Laurie stared at the post, sparks of panic shooting off inside her in all directions.

Quickly, she fired off a reply.

> **@BeautyintheKitchen** Sorry, the recipe accidently had some chilli in it. But I'm sure it's OK.

> **@StyleFile** WHAT? How could you have been so stupid?!!!! I hoped it was only me having a reaction (saved by using my mum's proper skin cream last night, btw). You had better fix this. FAST.

> **@BeautyintheKitchen** On it. Am in History corridor if you want to be here?

> **@StyleFile** I'm not in school. Am at the orthodontist having my mouth guard fitted, so you're on your own.

Out of nowhere, Rizwana and Sophie grabbed her by the arm.

'Hey!' said Laurie. 'What's going on?'

'What's *going on*?' asked Rizwana. She looked agitated and angry. 'What's going on is that our skin has been burning all night from that serum thingy!'

'What?' Laurie's throat went dry.

Sophie yelled. 'My forehead is still smarting now!'

'So we need to know,' said Rizwana. 'What on earth was actually in it?'

Laurie's heart thumped and her knees mushed. What if she'd done something terrible and this really was a poisonous skin serum? *I know it was only tomato and chilli*, she thought. *But even so!*

Rizwana and Sophie had their hands on their hips.

Laurie tried to sound calm. 'Our products are made from stuff you can find in the kitchen . . .'

'You can find bleach in people's kitchens,' Rizwana exclaimed. 'Doesn't mean you should slap it on your skin!'

'No, of course not!' said Laurie, her heart beating. 'I meant things like tomatoes, and lemons . . .'

'Food, in other words,' said Zainab, who was just coming out of the History classroom with Emilia. She made a face at Rizwana. 'You knew what she meant.'

'What's happening?' said Emilia.

'We've seen lots of stuff on School Stories about a toxic face serum,' said Zainab. 'People seem really—

'Angry! Yes, we are, actually,' said Sophie. 'Mum's put aftersun on my little sister but even so . . .'

'Aftersun!' said Laurie.

That was it! That was exactly what they needed. They needed an After-Chilli! Laurie had a coconut yogurt in her lunchbox. Yogurt clings on to chilli and helps wash it away! Laurie almost sagged with relief – it was going to be OK.

'I can make you a free treatment to fix this,' she said. 'Meet me at the benches near the field.'

As they rushed outside, Laurie pinged out a message on School Stories for anyone who had tried Skin Warrior to come for the second part of their treatment. And then she asked her friends what they had in their packed lunch.

By the time she got to the benches, there was already a crowd. And Laurie's hands were shaking with nerves as she mashed Elliot's banana and Zainab's strawberries into her coconut yogurt, with the back of a spoon. She thinned it out with a splash of the camomile tea that Annie had in her flask.

'You're basically doing a beauty hack,' said Zainab encouragingly. 'Pretend you're doing one of your vlogs . . .'

'And everyone happens to be watching,' said Emilia.

'Please can you sit here, Rizwana?'

With her hands shaking, Laurie smoothed back Rizwana's shiny, black fringe, and then, with the back of her spoon in her other hand, she spread some of the mixture on her face.

'This is called Lassi Rescue,' she said. 'It soothes and cools your skin, after it's had an invigorating, intense treatment like Skin Warrior.'

'Actually feels really nice,' said Rizwana, who looked a lot calmer. She was looking at her phone. 'And Charley says it's exactly what we need.'

Laurie flicked her screen.

> **@StyleFile** Skin Warrior is like the big guns of serum. So relax and find @BeautyintheKitchen on the field for some aftercare. She knows what she's doing!

Oh phew, thought Laurie, *that's definitely going to help me here*.

'Me next,' said Sophie.

After that, more girls had turned up, having seen

Charley's post, and wanted it done too. Rizwana snapped a selfie and posted it on her School Stories account.

'Rinse it off in a few minutes,' said Laurie. 'But don't worry, this is very gentle. The only danger is going to your next class looking like someone's thrown a smoothie over you.'

'Not a good look, to be fair,' said Rizwana.

'It was really full on, that Skin Warrior stuff,' someone said.

'Yeah, right,' sniggered a boy in Year 10, who was wearing a hooded parka, even though it was summer term.

'I'd like to see you try it,' Emilia whispered to Annie, who was standing next to her. Annie giggled.

'Oi, I heard that,' said the hooded-parka boy. 'Got any left?'

'No!' said Laurie, quickly. The last thing she wanted was for anyone else to use the fiery mixture. She knew it was wrong to waste food, but in this case, surely it made sense to get rid of the rest of the stuff.

'I have!' Sophie pulled out her pot.

'Seriously! There's no need for anyone to use the supercharged stuff!' said Laurie. 'Let's forget it!'

But it was too late. There were at least a dozen people pushing forward, saying that they wanted to have a go.

'Me first,' said Hooded Parka.

'Only leave it on a minute, everyone!' shouted Laurie. 'In fact, thirty seconds, max!'

But that made things worse.

'I can do longer than thirty seconds!' boasted a girl in Year 8. 'Pass the pot.' She had auburn hair scraped back with a glittery clip that said FEELINGS. Laurie didn't know her name, but she didn't look like someone to mess with.

'Challenge accepted,' said Hooded Parka.

He put his hood down, splashed his face with the serum, and held his phone up. 'I'm live streaming this on School Stories,' he told everyone. 'Hashtag FlamingFaceChallenge.'

He lasted about a minute and a half before he threw

his water bottle over his face. 'That was even tougher than having my face caked with mud on that Duke of Edinburgh hike last year!'

FEELINGS, however, made it to one minute fifty, which was hailed as the new super-endurance record. After that, it got really competitive, with loads of people trying to smash her time.

Laurie's heart was racing, and she couldn't wait until the bell rang for afternoon lessons. It was all a bit much. Fast forward to home time, though, and the hashtag was more hectic than she could have imagined. Laurie was desperately hoping Charley wouldn't flip her lid when she saw how Skin Warrior was being used – would she mind being the face behind a chilli mask rather than a premium skin product?

'Look at this!' shrieked Emilia, as she and Zainab walked Laurie to her bus stop. She threw her screen in front of Laurie's face. 'Ben Kalu's done the Flaming Face Challenge!'

There was a little clip that zoomed into Ben's cheeks

and then caught him smiling directly at the camera, his head backlit by the sun. He'd managed just under two minutes and the post had already had nearly thirty likes and shares.

And all the likes and shares were translating into real sales. Laurie couldn't believe how many orders were flying in.

Laurie's phone buzzed, and she swiped to see a direct message from Charley.

> **@StyleFile** Go, you! The #FlamingFaceChallenge rocks! Now that's what I call a cult product.

It wasn't until the weekend that Laurie got around to making the perfume. It had been a frantic Friday night making Skin Warrior – orders were flying in – and trying to keep up with homework (she didn't want Elliot getting ahead) and helping Fern with ideas for the March 4 Climate.

But on Sunday afternoon, Laurie had asked Fern

if she'd help mix up some perfumes. Fern had been pleased, as it was one of her favourite jobs, and Laurie was glad they were doing it together.

They'd spent about an hour shaking up rose petals, watermelon seeds, and lime peel and mixing them into perfume in the kitchen. Then they'd thrown the picnic rug under the magnolia tree in the front garden – it was a sunny, warm afternoon – and sat down to film a little clip to promote the new scent.

Laurie started by spraying water on to a milky white and pink petal, which Fern was holding. Fern tipped it, so the droplets sparkled in the sun.

It looked great, so Laurie posted it to School Stories:

> **@BeautyintheKitchen** Sniffing out your @T-Dates is FUN but stinky! After you've had a go, come and try our new fragrances! Double tap if you want to find your perfect perfume match.

'If I promote the T-Dates business at the same time as mine, we can both do well,' she told Fern.

Laurie tagged Charley into the post.

Within a second, there was a reply:

> **@StyleFile** Those hands in the photo? They're! So! Cute!

Laurie didn't show it to Fern. It would only wind her up.

'Oh, I forgot to tell you, Lau,' said Fern, sounding excited. 'Geoff the Garbage Chef has done a new vlog about his food waste challenge.'

'What now?'

Fern giggled. 'Get this. He goes into cafes and restaurants to show how much food is being left on the plates.'

Laurie rolled her eyes. 'Right.'

'And then, when the people have gone from the table, Geoff sits down and eats whatever they've left on their plates!'

Laurie did a double take. 'That's disgusting!'

Fern rested her head on Laurie's shoulder. 'In one restaurant, he has onion rings and chips! Then he goes into another and has a load of biryani, oh you should see it, Lau!' She giggled. 'He even finishes someone's pancakes. Someone had left a scoop of ice cream untouched. Can you believe that?'

'No! Who would leave ice cream?'

Fern sat up. 'So he's set up this new challenge, only for dedicated garbage guzzlers . . .'

'Go on.'

'. . . to go into cafes and restaurants and see if they can eat enough food for a proper meal from free leftovers.'

'That is wrong,' Laurie shook her head. 'That is so wrong.'

Fern paused, and then said in a casual voice, 'Mum and Dad thought they might try it.'

'What?' Laurie jerked up in shock. 'Eat off people's plates?' Her stomach did a triple somersault. 'What if someone sees them?'

'Geoff says not to worry about that,' Fern said. 'No one is looking at anyone really. He says that we worry that people are judging us and staring all the time but they're really not.'

'Maybe not if you're old but . . .' Laurie threw a confetti of tiny petals over Fern. 'I think Geoff should go back in time to his high school canteen, eat off other people's plates, and come back and tell us the reaction he got.'

Fern laughed. 'Good point.'

'Hiya!' Radzi was coming down the lane. He was wearing a hat that Laurie hadn't seen before. A felt cap, which really suited him.

'I was telling Lau about Geoff's restaurant challenge,' said Fern.

Radzi laughed. 'Polly mentioned that. They thought they'd go to the market because it's on one of the late night openings.'

Laurie sighed.

But it was good to see Radzi. Laurie liked the way he talked to them about Polly and Ed, instead of saying 'your mum and dad'. It made her feel much older, more like a friend than only a kid in the house he lived in.

Radzi threw himself down on the picnic rug and

picked up a bottle of the home-made perfume. He started to roll it between his hands. 'There's that central area, where you can take whatever you've bought to eat. They reckon they'll have their choice of leftover noodles, pizza or burgers . . .'

'Total yuk!' said Laurie.

'And there's that new vegan Indian place, which is meant to be great, if they fancy finishing someone's balti . . .' Radzi laughed. 'Step too far?'

Laurie nodded. 'Step towards food poisoning! You're so lucky that they're not your parents, Radz.' She took the perfume out of his hands and squirted a bit on his new hat.

Radzi gave Fern a nudge. 'What do you think about it?'

Fern laughed. 'I told them to bring us back some cakes.'

Later, that night, Laurie crawled into bed. Even though she was really tired, she still checked her phone. It had been fun hanging out with Fern and Radzi and the perfumes really were lovely. She'd gone for just one scent in the end, a combo of the smells that suited Emilia and Zainab. She just had to think of a cool name for it.

But the good vibes Laurie was feeling disappeared like a vanishing spell the second she checked her phone.

Charley had done a School Stories post of her own with an image of a beautifully lit close-up selfie. Charley had flowers in her hair and mini stick-on jewels on either side of her eyes.

> **@StyleFile** Your brand-new perfume launches on Monday. It'll be Week Two of the competition, people! Time to get serious. So, have some scents (see what I did there?!) and buy your bottle from **@BeautyintheKitchen** and say 'see ya' to stinky T-shirts!

Laurie's cheeks grew hot. *No!* She'd made it sound mean, like they were trying to compete instead of collaborate o this! She scrolled further down the messages.

@Lilliana Put me down for a bottle! My **@T-Dates** was so not my perfect match!

@T-Dates It is meant to be fun, you know.

@Rizwana Mine wasn't either. That thing's rubbish!

@Elise I know. How come I got Olly Hatton? I mean whaaaaat?!!!!!

@Orla And I wouldn't go out with Thomas Warburton if you paid me!!!!

@T-Dates And when you find your ideal match, the point is it isn't stinky!

@Elise It's total rubbish.

@Orla And so not science!

> **@ThomasWarburton** Same to you, Orla.

It totally looks like I started this. Laurie's heart thudded with fear. *The @T-Dates girls are in Year 9!! What are they going to think of me? What are they going to say?*

> **@T-Dates** We have the sweat of over half the school in our box.

> **@HarryEvans** @T-Dates is run by MI5, Don't you get it, people? They're collecting sweat so they can harvest your DNA. Don't do it! Don't be part of their database! #Resist.

> **@T-Dates** Hahahahahahaaha.

> **@LexiT** Oooooooo! **@T-Dates** and **@BeautyintheKitchen** went head to head, and here's what happened.

Lexi, the editor of the school magazine had strung

together a misleading montage of snippets and emojis between Laurie and @T-Dates. She'd completely twisted Laurie's words.

> **@LexiT** And of course School Stories has thoughts . . .

Lexi had then posted a load of the comments and they were getting lots of likes and shares. People were backing up T-Dates, and Laurie didn't blame them. Her face reddened as she scrolled down . . .

> **@AlfieB** who's got a #FlamingFace now, eh?

Me, obviously, thought Laurie. But her face was flaming with anger as well as embarrassment. Eyes watering, she sank her head into her pillow, which Fern had stuffed with dried lavender.

Her phone buzzed and Laurie reluctantly read the direct message from Charley:

@StyleFile Talk about whip up a controversy. LOL! Hope you're not doing your freaking-out face! Stay calm and make sure you have tons of products ready for Monday morning. Believe me, it's going to be BIG.

Chapter Eleven

@TheDisruptors It's Monday of Week Two, folks! By now you should have started to make sales! Remember, people love a story, so make sure they know why your product makes the world a better place!

As Laurie arrived at school on Monday morning, people were hanging around outside the building again before going to registration, and waving their wallets at her.

'Can I have one?' a girl in Year 8 asked.

'And me!'

'Me too!'

Girls were waving notes and pushing to get to the front of the crowd. Laurie put her satchel down. 'I'll get them out.'

'So, what did you say it was called?' someone asked.

Laurie paused. In her rush to get the perfume made she hadn't decided on a name.

Rizwana was there too. She whispered to Laurie. 'Does Charley wear this?'

Laurie rolled her eyes. 'Charley Wears This' should be their tag line.

'Here's Charley!' someone shouted.

Laurie's head jerked round – like everyone else's did – at the magnetic vision of Charley appearing on the field. What could she call this scent? Something that sounds like 'Charley' would probably sell well. But what?

Captivating?

Call the Shots?

'I am beyond picky about perfume,' Charley was saying, and girls literally parted as she arrived. 'But this is literally AWESOME.' Charley sloshed it everywhere. She whispered into Laurie's ear: 'This had better not be full of chilli!'

'It's a strong-statement perfume,' she continued to the crowd. 'Not everyone could carry it off.' Everyone was hanging on to her words – it was like there was a force field around her. Laurie was beginning to think that Charley wasn't popular because she was nice.

'Bold, captivating but ultimately unattainable,' Charley was saying.

'That's the one I want!' said Elise, thrilled.

'And me!' shouted a girl in Year 10. 'Have you got another bottle?'

'Us first, please,' said Orla. She put her arm around Elise and pushed herself into the space in front of Laurie. She raised her eyebrows. 'We are the brand influencers.'

'So, can we have a free product to showcase?' said Elise.

'No! If we're selling it already, we don't need to showcase it,' Charley hissed. Their faces dropped and she quickly flashed them a smile. 'Want to come to mine at the weekend?'

They instantly cheered and started supporting Charley by saying how the smell was truly immense. And the next few minutes were a rush of sales. Laurie watched as Charley worked the crowd, giving each girl a compliment ('Wow, loving your bag!', 'You have to tell me where you got that hair clip!'). They swarmed towards her like wasps to a giant jam sandwich.

And then she came over to Laurie, picked up a strand of her hair and giggled. 'Why is your hair wet?' she whispered. 'Did you have to wash out the bin juice, after getting your breakfast?'

Laurie's eyes pricked with tears.

'Your face!' Charley burst out laughing. 'I was J-O-K-I-N-G. You really need to ease up.' Then she picked up two strands of Laurie's hair. 'Here's a neat hack,' said Charley. She twisted the pieces at the front and secured it with one of her own clips. 'There! When it's dry, you can unravel it and it'll fall into perfect mermaid waves.'

One of the girls tapped Laurie's arm. 'What did you say this perfume was called again?'

'Charisma,' said Laurie. 'It's called Charisma.'

*

Later on they had Spanish, and as Laurie, Zainab and Emilia walked to the Modern Languages department, they were talking about the competition.

'I'm so glad, by the way, that the T-Dates comments were all a misunderstanding.' Zainab looked at Emilia. 'We didn't really think you would be mean, but it looked . . .'

'Mean,' said Emilia. She finished a mouthful of brownie which she'd bought from some Year 8s. 'But things often do on School Stories, even when they're not meant to be, don't they?'

Laurie nodded. 'It felt awful.'

'Forget it!' Emilia said. 'Your products are awesome, Laurie, and I bet you a whole cake that you will be in first place.'

'Well, we've had a good start.'

Laurie said this in an easy-going tone. The last thing she wanted to do was show off or make them think beauty products were better than birthday doggy biscuits. And she was still feeling uneasy after that comment Charley made about bin juice. Imagine if anyone had overheard it?

Emilia laughed. 'Understatement!'

Zainab carried on in her teacher voice. 'T-Dates is bound to do well at the start because everyone's going to have a go. But most people won't go back a second time.'

'And those Year Eights who will fix any bike for you are doing well too, and they're promoting a clean, green way to travel to school, so that's good,' said Emilia as she frantically shoved in the last bite of brownie.

They were near the Modern Languages rooms now, where world maps and posters of scenes from Paris, Berlin, Madrid, Beijing and Rome were dotted on the walls. Laurie looked at the photos longingly. She thought of how amazing it would be to book a trip to France on the Eurotunnel for Fern, Radzi and her parents.

'By the way, Rizwana and Lucy are only charging three pounds a go for their mehndi decorations,' said Zainab to Emilia as she paced along. 'That's what I said I'd sell my tuition services for, and you said it was too low for the competition.'

'For a study group, yes! You can't sell volume for that kind of thing, Zain. Mehndi's different.' She held her arms out, which were covered in patterns. 'Everyone's gone for it.'

'Low cost, high volume.'

'Unlike yours, Laurie!' said Emilia. 'High cost, high volume.'

Laurie flushed. 'I know it's way too much! I didn't set the price . . .'

'High exposure too,' added Zainab.

'And high fashion,' said Emilia. She flicked Laurie's hair, playfully. Laurie still had the twists of hair clipped up at the front, secured with one of Charley's clips. She'd kept them in for ages, so she felt a twinge of annoyance at how Emilia had loosened them.

Was Laurie imagining it, or had Zainab rolled her eyes when Emilia mentioned her hair? She quickly tried to move the subject on. 'How about we set aside this lunchtime for the doggy bags?'

'I'd rather eat a school dinner,' said Emilia with a laugh.

'And that's saying something,' said Zainab, who always brought a packed lunch.

Laurie laughed. 'Obviously, I meant working on them. I can help you with packaging, maybe, if you like?'

'No need,' said Emilia.

'We're all sorted, thanks,' Zainab said. She pulled an expression that Laurie couldn't quite understand.

'Or I could help bake some? Mrs Lundy says we can use the Food Tech room after school. We just have to let her know we'll be in there.'

Zainab spoke casually. 'We did them last night, actually, at Em's.'

'Took us half the night,' said Emilia, with an awkward laugh. 'We had to have a sleepover, in the end.' She looked at Laurie. 'But it wasn't planned or anything,' she said quickly. 'Or we would have . . .'

'And the biscuits are still not that good, you know! We

won't make anything like as much money as you will,' said Zainab. 'Not in a zillion!'

'Well, we definitely won't if you keep putting carrot peelings in them,' said Emilia, giving Zainab a friendly shove.

'It's not my fault!' She burst out laughing, and shoved Emilia back. 'We don't all have twenty-twenty vision, like you do. I bet you couldn't tell what was grated veg and what was peelings either, if you'd gone and left your glasses in Pizza Plaza . . .'

Laurie's glow began to fade away.

Zainab blushed deep red when she saw Laurie's face. 'We only went there . . .'

'Because there was nothing in the fridge at mine,' said Emilia. She played with the pink strands of her hair. 'Apart from rice pudding, and I did sort of kick up a fuss about having that for dinner again, so Mum took us for an early tea.'

'Just kind of an energy fill-up, basically, so we could get on with . . .' said Zainab. She muttered something about how it was an impromptu dough balls and salad, and how, in fact, they hadn't even had pizzas, come to think of it, and then trailed off.

'Anyway!' Emilia put on a bright smile. 'You OK?'

'I'm fine!' Laurie forced a laugh. 'Why wouldn't I be?'

CHAPTER TWELVE

The surprise of going from the ordinary bread and dairy-free butter of her life, to the glittery fame of working with Charley, was so enormous that Laurie kept having to remind herself that it was really happening.

Girls who had never given Laurie a second glance in their lives were talking to her in the corridors and messaging her. Did she have anything to make their hair type shine the way Charley's did? Did she have any more of the original batch of Skin Warrior because the girl with the FEELINGS hair clip still held the record?

It wasn't only Lower School girls, either, there were

boys, sixth-formers, even teachers. And her phone buzzed non-stop. She'd taken to carrying it with her everywhere – even upstairs. It was late now – past ten o'clock, on a Thursday night – and Laurie was lying in bed, trying to sleep.

It had been a full-on tea. Not the food – turtle bean burgers and salad – but the discussion. Loud, with everyone interrupting, and Fern's hands getting so animated that she sent the French vinaigrette flying.

One of the librarians where Laurie's mum held her Cook & Book groups had posted about the waste food snacks that would be available at the March 4 Climate. It was meant to be a positive way to help the Larksies. But she'd tagged some major supermarkets into it, and now some of them were fighting back on the #Foodwaste hashtag and saying it was irresponsible to hand out waste food.

It had made Laurie's parents and Fern more resolute than ever, but gave Laurie pangs of worry.

She was lying in the dark now, trying to focus on the

positives. She listened to Fern's soft breathing in the bunk below her. And she thought about the plants on the walls, dropping their scents in the darkness.

The LED lamps around the house dimmed at night, which gave everywhere a soft glow, and Laurie loved being in their botanical bedroom, with the rows of camomile, lavender and roses on the walls.

It was only the second week of the competition, but Laurie felt like her life had changed beyond recognition. Talk about engage, inspire and influence! But she did have a sad, squeezing feeling in her chest when she thought about Zainab and Emilia going off together. Laurie suddenly remembered that she had promised them a bottle of Charisma for helping her with the quiz. Her heart thumped. Her list of worries seemed to be growing as the competition went on – feeling guilty that she hadn't given enough time to helping her parents and Fern with the March 4 Climate preparations, and frantically trying to keep up with her schoolwork. And she was bound to lose out to Elliot in next week's Science assessment because she'd hardly done any revision.

Laurie sat up with a start as her phone buzzed. Charley was posting new messages about the competition. *She never switches off*, thought Laurie, reading the post.

> **@StyleFile** Get ready to kick bad skin to the kerb! It's time to bring out your natural glow. A new product for a new you coming later this week. Watch this space!

Laurie's heart began to beat faster. She grabbed some of the lavender from the walls and took a deep, calming sniff. Why on earth was Charley announcing a new product without talking to her about it first?

Slipping out of bed, she went downstairs to the kitchen and put a little orange pan on the stove to make some gingerbread milk. Laurie warmed the soya milk until it frothed, sprinkled in some sugar and a shake of ground ginger, mixed spice and cinnamon, and poured it into a mug. She took a gingerbread face mask – with yogurt and spices – out of the fridge and went upstairs to run a bath.

As the taps were going, Laurie looked in the mirror. All the extra hours spent perfecting her beauty products had given Laurie even more time to try them out herself. With a bit of Skin Whisperer (the non-Flaming Face version) every day, she couldn't help but notice how smooth and clear her skin was looking.

Laurie's parents wouldn't let her put selfies on School Stories. But if they did, Laurie reckoned she'd have the courage not to use a filter. *Well, not right now*, she thought, grinning to herself as she applied the face mask. She soaked it into her cheeks, chin and forehead, wrapped her head in a towel, and threw some home-made chocolate bath crumble into the water. Laurie leaned back against the end of the bath. She shut her eyes and swirled her hands by her side, wafting the chocolatey bubbles around.

This is what I need, she thought, trying to ignore the ton of homework she still had and all the products she had made. If it hadn't been for Radzi and Romy (who had come round for dinner) helping her to make that Saxon shield for the Battle of Hastings in History class, she would be very behind right now.

Though she'd also had to do fifty times-table questions, the Science revision, and had to rewrite the ending of one of her favourite books for English homework (Laurie had chosen *I Capture the Castle*). They really piled on the homework in Year 7 . . .

But there was no time to obsess further. Her phone was going off again.

Laurie wiped her hands and grabbed it, accidently swiping it as she lifted it up – and seeing Charley's face appear on the screen.

Argh!

Laurie's heart shot skywards.

She could hear Charley screaming with laughter.

Oh. My . . .

Laurie had answered a video call. That was Charley – in real life!

She plunged herself under the bubbles so only her

head was visible to Charley. 'Help!'

'Stop yelling!' said Charley's face on the screen. 'I can see you're in the bath! Which is *hilarious*, by the way, but stop the freaking. I can't see your hairy legs from here.'

Laurie tried to get her breathing back to normal. 'I didn't mean to answer a call like this!'

Charley was sitting in her bedroom with her knees tucked under a throw. She was wearing a soft-pink sweater, on-trend pyjama bottoms, and her hair was rolled into a headband halo. *Her hair really is everything*, thought Laurie. *All hail the hair*.

Charley laughed. 'What is that you're in, by the way, a muddy puddle?'

'Chocolate crumble.'

'Looks like you're literally lying in a hot chocolate. So, listen, I've been thinking about our social media. The posts aren't bad, but we need something more . . . relatable? Beauty vlogs, probably. Some really killer content.'

Killer content?

Laurie thought of the Beauty YouTubers she'd watched, with their sunny lives, chirpy hyped-up voices and pristine white bedrooms, so airy and light they could be made from candyfloss. And their 'OMG, it transformed my skin!' #DefyYouToResist reviews of products . . . that then sold out in seconds . . .

Charley had a point.

'So,' said Charley. 'We need to create some buzz around the content and we need to finalize our product range. Did you hear that they've set the school sale for Sunday the tenth? They had to switch it from the Saturday. Something about a clash with the school orchestra.'

Laurie sat up suddenly and hot chocolatey water whooshed up the sides of the bath.

'But that's the day of the March for Climate! I'm supposed to be going on it with my family, and—'

'And the sale will be tons more fun!' Charley giggled. 'Plus, you're doing your bit for the climate by selling home-made beauty products, aren't you?'

Laurie's stomach clenched. She wasn't sure her family would see it like that. But Charley wasn't interested in her worries. She was going off on one about something that she called the 'black hole of scrolling'. Laurie sighed. She would have to think of something. Maybe she could sell lots of products in the morning, and go to the march later?

She zoned back into Charley.

'. . . There are too many products to choose from on your Beauty in the Kitchen account. People go through it and they're thinking, *Urgh, so many recipes, I can't be bothered to look through them all. My pain!* We only need three,' she went on. 'Skin Warrior is doing well and so is Charisma. All we need to do is think of one more absolute fail-safe seller. Think about what every girl wants . . .'

'Clear skin?'

'We've already got Skin Warrior for that.'

'A zit-zapper that really works?'

Charley stopped dead. 'That's exactly what I was thinking!'

Laurie smiled.

'So, what's your best product for that?'

Laurie thought for a moment. 'I've got a recipe for polenta and maize flour with syrup – a vegan one, like agave. The grains gently buff and brighten skin and dry your spots out, while the syrup leaves you smelling like a toffee popcorn dream, or at least, that's how Fern described it.'

'You know your skincare, don't you?' said Charley, grudgingly impressed. 'Do you know all the recipes off by heart?'

'I love this one. All you have to do is spread it all over your face and gently rub it in, and ta-da, blemish-free skin! Well, in a few days. Plus, we've got lots of polenta – we got a sack from the health food shop when it was out of date. And I have syrup and flour, so it won't cost anything.'

Laurie squirmed down further under the bubbles. She wished she hadn't gone and mentioned the out-of-date polenta.

'An authentic new product for zero extra pounds

that clears your spots? Uh, yeah, I'll take it! But back to authentic content. Think about it. Nothing sells a product as well as a girl with acne showing that it clears her skin.'

'Of course,' said Laurie, trying to match Charley's serious tone.

'How about if you had a video, say, of a girl applying the product to her problem skin, doing the whole "before" bit, and then did a fast forward to a week later, and her skin had a soft, pretty flush? For a name, we could call it something like Zit Zap – although there are lots of products called that kind of thing.'

Charley pulled the sleeves of her soft-pink sweater over her hands and looked thoughtful. 'Spot Corn?'

Laurie winced. 'Great start, but sounds like a product for your feet.'

'You try then!'

Laurie rippled a hand in the chocolately water. 'OK, well, it smells of toffee popcorn, and you buy it because you want to get rid of spots, so, how about . . . Off You Pop?'

'That's like something a parent says to a toddler when they have to go out of the room!'

There was a pause. Finally Laurie said tentatively, 'Toffee Pops?'

Charley giggled, and in a sing-song voice, like a radio jingle, she said: 'Say goodbye to your spots . . . with Toffee Pops!'

'Love it!'

'You came up with the name. You're a genius!'

Laurie tingled for a second. It was hard to resist Charley when she said things like that; to not want to impress her. But it was impossible to tell if she was going to say 'You're a genius!' or 'You are insane!'

'So, who can we ask to do the video?'

'The twins!' said Charley suddenly. 'My cousins Isabelle and Isla are identical. Izzy's got acne and Isla hasn't. And no one at school knows them. They've recently had to move to a cold, empty place in the middle of the Scottish Highlands.'

In her head, Laurie could hear a blast of bagpipes as

she imagined two girls striding across the heather. *This could be good. Really good.*

'They can do a super-fast vlog, with Izzy applying Toffee Pops, and then Isla taking it off, showing us blemish-free skin. If we send them the recipe, they could make it themselves and have it done asap.'

Laurie suddenly felt uncomfortable. 'But that would be lying, wouldn't it?'

Charley laughed. 'It'll be advertising. Content! All beauty companies do that! None of those "clinically proven" claims by beauty vloggers stack up.'

Laurie's cheeks began to colour. 'The whole point of Beauty in the Kitchen is that it's not a con. It's the opposite of that – things actually work and they're not packed with horrible chemicals. It's not like all those beauty companies that pretend you can have all-day glossy lips or bright white teeth in a few days . . .'

Charley pursed her lips and thought for a moment. 'Well, OK, Laurie. Do you believe in Toffee Pops?'

'Yes! But I know it doesn't work instantly.'

'OK. We'll say "some time later", not the next day, in the "after" bit. Would that make it more true?'

Laurie sighed. 'It's better, but—'

'Come on, Laurie! Toffee Pops is a zero-cost product for us, it's safe and all we need to do is get the message out there.' She flashed her magnetic grin. 'Trust me, this is exactly what we need to do.'

It was so hard to say no to Charley. She popped a chocolate bubble with her toe and wondered how bad it was to create content like this. Everyone knew that those glamorous posts on social media were staged. Charley knew so much more than her about selling and products. Laurie didn't even go into shops, so she felt she should trust Charley's judgement on this. She told herself not to listen to the nagging little voice inside her that said it was a bad idea. And really, was it any worse than what they were already doing – which was not telling people that the skin products they were slapping on their faces were made with leftovers, and even food from the bins? Laurie knew it was OK to use ingredients like that – more than OK, in fact, as it helped the planet – but wasn't that already false advertising?

'Izzy and Isla are bored stiff. Living up there, they hardly know anyone, and their home is really damp and cold. They'll be so pleased if we ask them to create this.'

'OK . . .' Laurie said uncertainly. 'Shall we meet tomorrow and write a script for Isla and Isabelle?'

'No. Let them do their thing. It'll be way better than anything either of us can write.'

She still wasn't sure, but if she could help Charley's cousins have some fun with this video, *maybe* it was the right thing to do.

Chapter Thirteen

A few days later, Laurie, Zainab and Emilia were walking past the Science Block when Laurie opened her bag. 'I nearly forgot!' She pulled out two bottles of Charisma. 'These are for you.'

Emilia and Zainab looked like they'd unwrapped a very disappointing Christmas present.

'What's wrong?' asked Laurie.

Zainab pulled an apologetic face and said, 'Sorry, Laurie, this is great and everything. Really kind of you. But . . .'

'We thought you meant we could have one of your Puddings Perfumes!' said Emilia.

'Every day you smell of strawberry jelly or ginger cake and custard,' Zainab said. 'It's like being friends with the puddings trolley.'

'And we love it! I've been secretly hoping you would make me a bottle of blackcurrant crumble.' Emilia shook her head. 'Doesn't matter though,' she said quickly. 'I'm sure we'll love this one too.'

'Of course,' said Zainab. 'It's very . . . sophisticated.'

Laurie grinned. 'Hand them over!' She threw the bottles back into her bag. 'I'd much rather make you a proper one!'

Laurie was still feeling cheery later when she was on her way to the library. She and Charley had arranged to meet there after school so they could watch the vlog together.

But when Laurie arrived, Charley was giggling at her phone, which instantly made her uneasy. Had Charley screen-grabbed their call last week and posted photos of Laurie in the bath? *Oh, don't be stupid*, Laurie told herself. *Get a grip!* She was probably watching the World's Funniest Kittens on YouTube.

'Don't look so worried.' Charley shifted up the sofa

and unwrapped a chocolate bar. They weren't supposed to eat or drink in the library, but Charley Keating-Sloss just did whatever she liked.

Laurie looked around. There was hardly anyone in the library apart from a few sixth-formers, and a bunch of Year 8s and 9s who were unlucky enough to have to go to homework club. She pulled out her flask. Her mum had filled it with oat milk.

Charley laughed. 'What a rebel!'

Laurie tried to look as if she couldn't care less. She checked none of the sixth-formers were looking at her before she glugged down some hot milk so quickly she nearly burnt her throat.

Charley pressed PLAY.

The opening scene showed Isabelle sprawled on a four-poster bed in a room full of antique furniture. She was wearing stripy pyjamas, thick socks and a sapphire choker.

'I have Good Skin Days and Not So Good Skin Days, and I've Got Acne Get Me Out of Here Days. I've stopped trying everything people with well-behaved pores tell me. Only *I* really know what works for *me*,' Isabelle said directly to the camera. She picked up a silver goblet and took a sip of water.

Laurie's eyes widened. Isabelle was funny, friendly, she had great eyebrows, and she ought to be on Charley's StyleFile: '*Nightwear*: £90. *Heirloom sapphire choker*: priceless (but estimated price, £1.5m). *Fabric throw*: nineteenth-century, on display at the V&A, London. Not for sale.' But she looked at Charley in confusion.

'I thought you told me things were hard for Isabelle and Isla, that they were living in a nightmare place?'

'It is a nightmare! Izzy is freezing. Look at her!'

On the vlog, Isabelle had picked up a shawl and wrapped it around her shoulders.

'That fabric looks valuable. I know it sounds mad, but honestly, I saw a silk shawl like that in an exhibition once. Zoom into it!'

Charley paused the vlog and enlarged the image.

'Yes!' said Laurie. 'That's the same! It's either a vintage

style or it's a genuine antique from . . . I don't know exactly but, maybe mid-nineteenth century?'

'LOL!' said Charley. 'Seriously, though, poor Izzy and Isles! That's so typical of my aunt and uncle. They hardly ever buy them new things. And they live in one of the oldest inhabited homes in Scotland.'

'A castle?'

'It might as well be. It's draughty and damp. There's no central heating, no carpets, no hot showers . . .' Charley ticked each one off on her fingers.

Charley pressed PLAY again, and they both peered at the screen to see Isabelle absent-mindedly rocking a carved oak cradle. There was a golden retriever asleep in it.

'And that dog's bed is ancient,' moaned Charley. 'As in, it belonged to Bonnie Prince Charlie or someone.'

If only teleportation had been invented! If Isabelle and Isla weren't happy living in their castle, then Fern and Laurie would have been more than willing to trade. It was typical of Charley to act as if valuable, historical things were nothing. They didn't have a clue!

But there was no denying that Isabelle was a natural in front of the camera. And Laurie did laugh at a bit when she put tiny heart-shaped stickers over her spots and said that some days even cover-up zit stickers weren't enough. Then she went on to talk about how light the consistency of Toffee Pops was while she applied it to her face.

Laurie shifted a little further along the sofa. She was struggling to work out what she thought of this vlog. But she carried on watching as Isabelle explained that she was off to her secret den while Toffee Pops did its thing.

A second later, there was a blast of music and a bookcase swung open to reveal Isla, wearing stripy pyjamas and a big blue jumper. 'All I can say is wow!' said Isla. 'My zit-uation has completely gone. Toffee Pops totally rocks!'

Charley held her hand up for a high five. 'Trust me Laurie, this is what you call killer content.'

@StyleFile So-oooooo, we went looking for the perfect vlog to showcase our product. And we found it. Prepare for awesomeness. ♥ ♥ ♥ ♥ ♥ ♥

Chapter Fourteen

The next morning, in History, Laurie looked at the clock on the wall for the zillionth time. Ten to twelve. Twenty-five minutes until lunch.

If only this lesson was already in the past. Laurie couldn't concentrate today. Her eyes glanced at the clock again. How long until she could turn her phone on and see how well the vlog was doing on School Stories?

Emilia gave Laurie a nudge. 'You listening?'

'To Mr Patel talking about the disputed succession in 1066, or to you going on about whether you should ask Ben Kalu out?'

Elliot rolled his eyes. He sat on the same table as Laurie, Zainab and Emilia in History, along with a boy called Ned Jinks, who was using his voice for The Disruptors.

For two pounds, Ned would serenade anyone you liked. People were getting him to do things like sing to dinner ladies to get extra chips. And last week, Harry Evans paid him to sing an apology to Mr Henderson, the Geography teacher, because he'd forgotten to do his homework.

It was true that Emilia had been going on a bit. But she knew why. Before school, Emilia had sold some doggy birthday biscuits to Ben Kalu, and this was monumental, as it was the first time they'd actually spoken.

Laurie had missed the Big Moment because she had been in the Year 9 cloakroom, giving Charley some sachets of Toffee Pops, in case the vlog sparked some interest. A fact that Emilia had mentioned at least three times already.

Emilia leaned over the table. 'So, what do you think?'

Laurie paused. It wasn't as if she'd ever had a crush before. How was she meant to know what to do? 'I think Harold faced two invasions. One from the King of Norway . . .'

'Be serious. This matters to me, you know,' said Emilia, looking annoyed.

Ned exchanged an irritated glance with Elliot.

'The thing is,' Emilia whispered, 'instead of walking home tonight, I'm wondering if I should go to the fifty-three bus stop for a few minutes. That's where Ben gets his bus. If you two are there –' she looked at Laurie and Zainab – 'I might have the courage to talk to him again.'

Laurie bit her lip. 'Sorry, but I told Charley I'd make loads of our new Toffee Pops product tonight. I need to rush home and do it.'

'Never mind!' Zainab cut in. 'I'll be there!'

'What do you think I should say?' Emilia looked excited.

'Aw, c'mon,' said Elliot. 'Give it a break, Emilia. Some of us want to do well in this subject.'

Emilia flushed. 'I'll stop talking when you move that sweaty pebble.' She pushed it with the corner of her exercise book.

'Don't do that!' Elliot grabbed the pebble. 'I got it

out to show you, Laurie, that the pebble's eroding the bottom of my left foot, making it smoother than my right because I don't have a pebble in my right shoe.' He tapped it on the table. 'Thought it might be good for Beauty in the Kitchen?'

'Thanks,' said Laurie, looking unsure but not wanting to hurt Elliot's feelings. 'I'll have a think.'

Elliot beamed. He put his feet up on the table – double quick so he didn't get caught. 'And if you need to see the results . . .'

Laurie held her nose. 'No thanks!'

'Are you finished?' said Emilia, looking frustrated. '*As I was saying . . .*'

Ned's head jerked up. 'She's really getting on my—'

Just then, Laurie had an idea.

When the bell rang, she thrust a sachet of Toffee Pops into Ned's hands. People were squashing past them on the way out of the classroom, so it was all a bit rushed. But she managed to garble something about how she didn't have any money. 'So, will you take this in exchange for serenading Ben Kalu?'

Ned looked at it dubiously.

'It honestly works!' said Laurie. 'But please sing to Ben and see if he likes Emilia.'

'I'll try.'

Emilia threw her arms around Zainab in excitement. 'Seriously? Thank you, Laurie. Oh, Zain, let's go straight there as soon as the bell goes for the end of school!'

'Can't wait,' said Zainab heartily.

'You're welcome,' said Laurie quietly as she watched her friends run off together.

Laurie went to a bench in the far corner of the field and flicked on her phone. She nearly fell off the bench with excitement.

Already, the vlog had nearly sixty shares. Which was incredible, as everyone had been in school since nine in the morning and only the sixth-formers were allowed their phones on in the building. So to have sixty views already was amazing!

And the post about the vlog on Beauty in the Kitchen was getting shares, likes and comments.

One Year 9 girl had reposted the vlog, with the caption *Toffee Pops is a thing now and we NEED it*. And that post had got another twelve shares, which meant they were up to seventy-two views! Laurie flicked on to YouTube to double check the counter as her phone buzzed again.

> **@StyleFile** Just make sure you have the products ready! Reckon there'll be loads more orders and we need to fulfil them!

Laurie opened her flask and had a few sips of ginger cordial. It felt good. Who would have thought that she would be messaging the most popular girl in school? A week or two ago, she had never even spoken to her! And it wasn't as if she were stupid enough to think they were friends. Her heart thudded. Hopefully, asking Ned to serenade Ben Kalu would show Emilia and Zainab that they were still really good friends, even though she'd not spent much time with them recently. One good thing about the competition being over soon was they could get back to hanging out together more.

Laurie looked around. The air was warmer now it was May, and there was pink-tinged blossom on the apple trees. Laurie liked the way the trees were randomly scattered – because they hadn't been planted, they'd sprouted from discarded cores, chucked by students long ago. *I must tell Fern that!* thought Laurie. It was a great example of how food waste can be good.

If Laurie felt that the vlog was going well by lunchtime, she was gobsmacked when she checked her phone on the school bus that afternoon: 352 shares! And by the next day, it was off the scale entirely.

Toffee Pops had gone viral.

Chapter Fifteen

The vlog became the single most shared piece of content that Silverdale High had ever had on School Stories. It was a trillion times more popular than the #FlamingFaceChallenge or anything that competitors like T-Dates had done.

The orders for Toffee Pops were flying in. Laurie was worried about how she was going to make enough to fulfil all the orders, so Charley had suggested they create a waiting list. But that only seemed to make people want it more.

Laurie was scrolling School Stories while in her bedroom. It was Friday night, at the end of the second week of the competition and only two days since she and Charley had both posted the vlog – and it had taken on a life of its own. By now, she had no way of knowing the total shares because people had started new posts and reposts.

Laurie had a bounce in her step as she ran downstairs for tea. In fact, she was so happy about the response the vlog was getting that she showed it to the others.

Massive mistake.

Her dad was so shocked that he spat out his cannellini bean pasta. He got Laurie to play it again (once she'd wiped her phone) and pause at the bit where Isla appears with blemish-free skin. 'You've invented this, Lau?' he said, looking really impressed. 'Made this girl's spots go away?'

'Awesome vlog,' said Radzi. 'Did you write the script?'

'No, it was all Isabelle and her sis—'

'Hang about! Was that the polenta exfoliating mask we invented?' said Fern. 'Because if it was, how come I put it on my face last week and I've still got a spot?'

'Fern!' said Laurie. 'That's a chicken pox scar. And I told you to use vitamin E on it.'

'Looks like you've done a terrific job, Lau!' said

Laurie's mum. She helped herself to some more pasta. 'Seriously. Well done you. And now I know why we've gone through so much polenta!'

Laurie's mum and dad hadn't realized that Isabelle and Isla were the content creators. But Fern would know it wasn't real . . . that there's no such thing as zit-zapping polenta. Laurie felt a lump rising in her throat. They were going to be so disappointed.

In all the excitement, Laurie had forgotten that Toffee Pops didn't really work like the vlog said it did. It was a stupid advert making beauty claims that didn't stack up. The sort of advert the Larksies hated.

Laurie cleared her throat. 'The funny thing is—'

'You'll be off to work for . . . what's that's place that you like called again?' said her dad. 'The one with the shampoo bars and fizzy things? You know where I mean! You can smell it halfway down the high street.'

'That would be amazing,' said Laurie. 'And yes, I do love it. But the thing is—'

'And you will fulfil your big giant dreams!' Fern said.

She threw her arms out, and nearly knocked over the salad bowl. 'Of being a beauty billionaire, inventing new bubble bars and . . .'

And this is exactly why I shouldn't have told Fern my ambition, thought Laurie, her heart thundering. Because now her parents were going to say that being a beauty billionaire was somehow the same as being money-grabbing, spoiled and selfish.

Laurie's mum gave a disbelieving laugh. 'I don't think Lau wants that.'

'Why shouldn't I?' Laurie felt her cheeks get hot. 'It would mean I can give money away to help people, and support the things we believe in. Instead of scrimping and saving all the time . . .'

Mum looked hurt.

Laurie knew that she'd gone too far. She put her hand out on top of her mum's. 'I didn't mean to hurt your feelings! I didn't mean it like that! I meant—'

'There are other ways to help people,' said Fern conversationally. 'It's not only about giving away money.'

It was all right for Fern. Everyone knew her ambition was to be featured in the *Rebel Girls* books, and their parents found that incredibly impressive – they called her 'our little firecracker'. But just because Laurie wanted to be successful in a different way . . .

'Very true, Fern,' said Laurie's dad. 'And Lau, I agree that people should share their wealth and be kinder. But if there's one thing I know –' he waved his fork, with a piece of pasta hanging off the end – 'it's that having lots of money doesn't make you happy.'

'I don't want lots of money!' said Laurie.

'You just want the things you can buy with the money,' said Fern reasonably. 'And that vlog will help you sell Toffee Pops really quickly. You could actually put some sparkles across the screen, like you're waving a magic wand.'

'Fern, it's done now, so stop being annoying!'

Laurie's dad was still going on.

'. . . and I'm not saying that struggling for money makes you happy either, because in that case, life can be very tough. What I'm saying is—'

'We get the point,' said Laurie. She took a deep breath. She was going to have to tell them it was an advert, and she may as well get it over with. 'Can I just explain about how we did the vlog?'

But Fern butted in again. 'Anyway! You know Leon Matthews, who's on my lunch table?'

Everyone nodded. They'd heard the saga of lunches with Leon all term. He and Fern were good friends, but Leon was very traditional and teased Fern about her packed lunches.

'He was going on about how I'm going to turn into a vegetable because I only eat plants.'

'Still?' said Laurie's dad. 'Thought he'd be bored of that by now.'

'Don't tell me you gave one of your speeches about how we need to eat less meat and dairy to stop climate change?' said Laurie anxiously. 'I mean, I know that's true – I've never eaten either of them in my life! – but everyone thinks you're judgy if you go on about it . . .'

'He picked a piece of cucumber out of my rice salad and held it up in front of my face. And said, "You're going turn into a vegetable, you are!"'

Radzi looked appalled. 'Hope you told him a cucumber is a fruit?'

'What did you do?' asked Laurie, her stomach turning.

No matter how irritating her sister could be at times, Laurie hated to think of Fern having problems at school. She couldn't wait until Fern was at Silverdale High so that Laurie could look after her. They could even sit together at lunch.

'I picked the sausage off his plate.' Fern paused dramatically. 'It was dripping with gravy, by the way.'

'Bleurgh!' said Laurie.

'I waved it around, and I said, "Yeah, well, it's better than turning into a pig's bottom, like where this came from!"'

Laurie's parents burst out laughing, and Radzi had some kind of coughing fit.

Laurie's mouth dropped open. 'You are joking? You didn't actually say that, did you?'

'I did, I did!' said Fern, her eyes shining. 'Oh my gosh! You should have seen his face!'

'I can imagine,' said Laurie's dad.

Laurie shook her head. Weren't any of them worried about Fern losing all her friends or getting into trouble? 'Didn't you get told off?' she said.

'No!' said Fern. 'Well, I mean, Mrs Ravenhurst, the dinner lady, told me off for putting my hands in someone's dinner. But she told Leon off too! And she made us move tables. But who cares?'

Fern slung her arm around her mum's shoulder.

'Oh, Fern,' said Laurie's mum.

'Leon thought it was hysterical,' Fern went on. 'We had a right laugh in the playground later. He was pretending to be a pig and I kept on doing my "plant power" pose at him . . .'

'Well, good for you!' said Laurie's mum as she went to the oven, and came back with a raspberry crumble and a jug of oat-milk custard.

Laurie's dad started passing the bowls to everyone.

'Not much for me, please,' he said. 'We're going to walk into town and do Geoff's restaurant challenge later, aren't we, Polly?'

'Yes!' Laurie's mum looked excited.

'You're what?' said Laurie.

'Going to eat off people's plates in restaurants,' said Fern. 'I told you that! They're giving it a go at the market tonight.'

Laurie's spoon fell from her fingers and clattered noisily to the table.

'It's late night opening,' said her dad.

'Big helping for you, though,' said her mum, with a smile. She handed Laurie the jug. 'We need to celebrate, Lau. I've been worried that you look really tired – so please have an early night – but you seem to be doing so well.'

'Yes, well done,' said her dad. He poured on enough custard to fill a swimming pool. He looked up, his eyes proud and pleased. 'I really think you're on to something.'

'I've always loved the beauty products you and Fern

make,' said Laurie's mum. 'But I didn't realize they were quite so effective.'

'Mum! Please, stop it!'

'I was only saying . . .'

Everyone went quiet, spooning crumble into their mouths.

Fern screwed up her nose. 'Wait a minute, can you play the vlog again?' Her eyes were shining, like she'd made a monumental scientific discovery.

Laurie didn't want to put it on, but she grabbed her phone, hoping it would stop the conversation.

Fern put her face about a centimetre from the screen, and halfway through, her thumb hit PAUSE. 'I knew it!' She turned the screen around to the others, triumphantly.

Fern zoomed into a close-up of Isabelle's spotty face. She then flicked to the next shot. Isla was showing off her dewy skin.

She jumped off the chair in excitement. 'Can you see it?'

Laurie's parents shook their heads.

Laurie felt like the custard in her stomach was curdling. She should have known that Fern would work it out.

'In the first shot, the girl has three freckles on her nose . . .' Fern talked with such conviction and confidence she could give a prime minister a run for their money. 'Yet, in the second the freckles are gone. So, we must ask ourselves, why no freckles? And all I can think is . . .'

Radzi stood up. 'I'll get started on these dishes.'

'. . . that these girls are twins!'

Laurie's mum's head jerked around. She stared at Laurie.

Laurie felt her face go as red as the raspberry crumble. 'So? That's not a crime, Mum! They're Charley's cousins and—'

'So Charley's family knows about this?'

'I don't know! Her mum works away a lot.'

'So, they don't know she's posting fake content?' said Laurie's dad.

'It's an advert, Dad! It's not meant to be a hundred per cent accurate.'

Her mum sighed and looked at her sadly. 'Well, I'll tell you what does need to be a hundred per cent accurate. Our food waste snacks for the March for Climate. It's all very well you doing this competition, Laurie, but I want to see a lot more of you helping out now, with preparations for the march.'

'Agreed,' said Laurie's dad, as he left the kitchen, shaking his head.

Laurie's eyes filled with tears. She put her head down on the table and wrapped her hands behind her neck, so her elbows covered her ears. *And if you think that went badly, imagine what they're going to be like when you tell them you can't make it to the march.*

While her parents were out, Laurie, Fern and Radzi stayed in the sitting room. Laurie had done her homework, made some more Toffee Pops, and now she was utterly exhausted and lying on the sofa.

They were watching *Doctor Who*. This was because Fern had to watch it because otherwise Neisha and Alex, who were in her class at school, wouldn't let her play with them at breaktime. Neisha and Alex were obsessed with *Doctor Who* and Fern was obsessed with being their friend.

But Fern hated *Doctor Who*, because she found it really scary. So Radzi watched it with her, fast forwarding bits, and explaining other parts so she knew enough to convince Neisha and Alex that she could play with them.

Laurie lay beside them. She was still a bit cross with Fern and feeling sick about how disappointed her mum and dad were, but in a way it was a relief that Fern had spotted the twins, because Laurie absolutely hated lying.

She let herself sink into the sofa and daydream. If the sales kept up like this, there was a very real chance they'd win the school competition and maybe even the overall competition too. They'd get the printer for the school. One day, they could be printing their own face packs, she thought, absent-mindedly checking her phone.

Charley had posted a clip of herself next to their range of skin serum, scent and spot zapper, on the side of a huge copper bath, in a gleaming white bathroom.

> **@StyleFile** Words can't describe how thankful I am for how much you love our range. This little dream of mine is coming true and I can't wait for the school sale #skincare #beauty #thedisruptors.

Laurie's chest tightened. It was hard not to stare at that photo: Charley looked like a celestial goddess. But it would be really nice if she would mention Laurie in the posts, and talk about 'their' dream rather than just hers.

The post was racking up the likes. Ben Kalu had reposted it, saying he was #InAwe. Laurie cringed. She thought again about the rumours that he liked Charley and she hoped – for Emilia's sake – that it wasn't true.

Not that Emilia had mentioned him for a few days. Ned's bus stop serenade had been a complete disaster – Ben and his mates had presumed it was a joke. Ben had actually slapped Ned on the back and shouted, 'Ha ha ha! Good one!' before jumping on the bus, without even finding out who Emilia was.

'Ow!' Fern accidently stood on Laurie's hair, jerking her back to real life, and not her phone.

'Sorry, Lau. Didn't mean to do that.'

Laurie looked at the television. They were on a fast-forward bit of *Doctor Who*. Fern was picking cherries from the tree and dangling them over her ears.

'Do these look real?' she asked, pulling back her hair and shaking her head until the cherries swung violently.

Radzi smiled. 'They're rubies, right?'

Fern grinned. 'And now for my next trick.' She pulled a packet of biscuits out from down the side of the sofa.

'Fern!' said Laurie. 'Where did you get those?'

'I went garbage guzzling after school.'

'What?' Laurie was immediately worried. 'I didn't know you were doing that. I thought you were waiting until next weekend to get some stuff . . .'

'I know! But I couldn't wait, Lau! We were going past the shops near the park and the bins looked full and so I asked Mum if I could go for a bin dive on my own.' Fern looked excited. 'On my own! She parked the car around the corner and—'

'Wait. Mum parked around the corner and let you?'

'I wanted to do this by myself.'

Laurie sighed. It seemed like Fern had it really easy. It had taken ages for their mum to let Laurie go as far as the park by herself when she was in Year 5, and she still got anxious about Laurie getting the bus by herself, even though she was in Year 7. She was always messaging 'Please be careful crossing the roads' and 'Drink more water!' *But when it comes to Fern*, thought Laurie, *she's basically allowed to roam free.*

'Anyway, this was sticking out of the top.'

'What's the best-before date?' Laurie asked, picking up the box. 'Half the stuff in that shop is stale when it's on the shelves, let alone the bins . . .'

'Oh, crack 'em open!' said Fern, grabbing the box back.

She pulled apart the plastic packet, wrinkling her nose in disgust. Then she stuffed a biscuit into her mouth and pretended to collapse on the floor.

'Oh, ha ha ha,' said Laurie.

'Pass them over,' said Radzi. 'They're going back into the Tardis.'

They settled back down on the sofa and between the three of them they finished the packet as the Doctor saved the world.

The key turned in the lock.

'That's early.' Radzi raised his eyebrows.

'Did you get any cake?' shouted Fern.

Laurie's dad put his head around the sitting-room door. 'It wasn't a resounding success.'

'We got asked to leave the restaurant,' said her mum.

'The manager was sympathetic,' said her dad, taking off his shoes. 'Says he doesn't like leftovers either and agrees there's an issue with portion control.'

This sounds bad, thought Laurie.

Her mum flopped on to the sofa. 'That's why we

headed there first, because Geoff says there's so much leftover rice. Apparently a third of biryani never gets eaten.'

'It was a miscalculation, really,' said her dad.

Laurie's palms began to sweat. 'A miscalculation?'

He sat down. 'We found a plate of chana masala at an empty table. It was practically untouched, and so, we dug in . . .'

'It was absolutely delicious!' said her mum.

'But it turned out that the guy whose meal it was had popped to the loo,' Laurie's dad continued. 'He hadn't abandoned it at all. In fact, he was still in the market hall! So, when he came back, there was a bit of a fuss . . .'

'And that's when you got chucked out?' Laurie spluttered.

'I wouldn't say chucked,' said her dad. 'We left voluntarily, Lau. We apologized to everyone. It was all very polite.'

Laurie's mum nodded. 'Cut a long story short, we ended up paying for the man's meal to show everyone how sorry we were.'

'Like I said, a misunderstanding,' said her dad.

'Funny, really,' said her mum. 'You should have seen his face!'

She started doing an impression of the man finding them eating his chana masala. She stormed across the room, with her face pulled into a ludicrously shocked expression. Her dad pretended to hand back half a chapatti.

Fern cracked up laughing.

'Bet you won't be eating out again in a hurry,' said Radzi lightly.

'This isn't a joke, Radzi!' said Laurie suddenly. 'How would you feel if your mum and dad had been caught troughing someone else's food?'

'Laurie!' said her mum, looking cross. 'Don't be rude, please.'

'Rude?' Laurie's felt her cheeks flame. 'Mum! You've just eaten someone else's dinner. That's *rude*!'

'Good point,' said Fern.

'Yes, thank you,' said Laurie's mum sharply. She looked at the clock on the wall and pointed at Fern. 'Pyjamas, teeth, bed.'

Fern walked as slowly as possible to the sitting-room door.

When she finally opened it, Radzi took the opportunity to make a sharp exit. Before he left, he looked at Laurie. 'Try not to worry. The chances of anyone from school having seen the . . . incident . . . are pretty much zero.'

Laurie's heart slammed. Pretty much zero was not the same as zero.

'What if they did, though?' she said as Fern left. 'If Charley finds out, she'll freak! I'm not messing around here! This is really important.'

'I didn't say it wasn't,' said her mum, eyeballing Laurie.

'No one will ever buy one of my products again if they hear about what you've done. And Zainab and Emilia won't want to be my friends either if I've been linked to a crime!'

Laurie's dad ran his hand through his hair. 'A

misjudged mouthful of chickpeas doesn't make us criminals.'

Her mum flopped back down on the sofa. 'There was hardly anyone around, Lau.'

'It only takes one person to see it, video it,' said Laurie, panicking, 'and put it on School Stories and—'

'Surely people would see the funny side,' said her dad.

'*What* funny side would that be, Dad?' said Laurie. She jumped up, feeling hurt and angry. 'There is no funny side! This food waste thing, it's gone too far! Don't you ever think about how what you do might affect me?'

'We're constantly thinking about how our behaviour affects you and Fern,' snapped Mum. 'For goodness sake, that's why we're taking you on the March for Climate!'

'Actually, you're not!'

Laurie could feel waves of anxiety rising in her chest as she stared at Mum and Dad's shocked expressions. But there was no going back now. 'The school sale is on the same day as the march. So I can't go.'

'The sale?' Mum looked furious. 'I'm sorry, Laurie, but you'll have to tell them you've already made a commitment to doing something else that day.'

'Which is very important,' said Dad. 'This is about the future, for you and—'

'This is about the future too, Dad. My future!'

Mum and Dad flashed their eyes at each other.

Dad did a huge sigh. 'Sometimes as parents we have to make unpopular decisions . . .'

Laurie yanked the door open. 'And sometimes, I can make decisions for myself, thank you very much!' She ran upstairs, knowing that her parents would be going on about how disappointed they were that she would choose to sell products at school rather than go on the march with them, and that it was *because* they cared about what affected Laurie that they were so committed to action on climate change.

That's not the same thing at all, thought Laurie, burying her face in the pillow. She knew that they were trying to save the planet but . . .

Everything was out of control. Laurie was scared that Fern was bin diving on her own and that her parents would get into trouble at the march. Her homework was piling up, as were the orders for Toffee Pops and Skin Warrior, and she felt absolutely exhausted with the worry that she could lose both her friends and the competition. And she had a horrible feeling that something even worse was going to happen.

CHAPTER SIXTEEN

> **@TheDisruptors** It's Monday of the final week, everyone! You've got five school days left to sell, sell, sell, and then it's the weekend Event – where friends and family can come and boost your sales. Don't waste a minute, folks. This time next week, the winner will be announced.

Laurie was still feeling awful about letting down her family, by not going on the march, when she was at school on Monday. That morning, she and Fern had eaten a silent bowl of cereal together and Laurie was worrying about it as she wandered on to the field at break. She bumped into Annie and her friend Zoe, who were showing Zainab and Emilia their newly bought personalized jogging pants.

'They're sooo cool,' said Zainab. 'The stitching is perfect.'

Annie and Zoe had both gone for matching inky blue joggers, with their names embroidered in crimson stitches down the legs.

'They've got charcoal joggers, or you can have them in soft grey. They've got loads of threads, so you can choose any colour for the stitching.'

Emilia ran her fingers over the stitches and said how great they were. Then she turned to Zainab and Laurie. 'Shall we get some?'

'Only if I can get them in blue with red stitching too!' said Zainab. She looked at Annie and Zoe. 'You don't mind?'

'Of course not!' said Annie and Zoe, practically in the same breath.

'I'll go for the same.' Emilia said.

'It can be a thing,' Zoe smiled. 'What do you think, Laurie?'

Laurie put her hands to her cheeks. She could feel the familiar beetroot colour flooding into them. It was bad enough trying to get money for hot chocolate.

But those joggers were expensive.

'You don't have to,' said Zainab, suddenly looking worried. 'If you've, you know . . .'

'Not got your purse,' finished Emilia.

Laurie searched for something good to say. If only she could come up with a spot-on reason that would explain why she never had any money. *I'm sick of feeling so awkward*, she thought. *I'm tired of waiting to be a beauty entrepreneur way off in the future. I need money NOW!*

Zoe looked worried. 'What's the matter?'

'Oh no! Have you lost your purse?' said Annie, who looked on the verge of tears at the thought. 'Nightmare! Was your bus pass in there too?'

'Do you need us to lend you anything?' Zoe threw the joggers into her bag, as if even the sight of them would distress Laurie. 'Because we could share our lunch . . .'

'No! Thanks, but no.'

Laurie's throat was closing up. She couldn't wait until the end of The Disruptors when she and Charley could split the money and go their separate ways.

Obviously, that didn't help her to buy the joggers now. But at least she could go the cafe for hot chocolate and buy Emilia something for her birthday next month.

'We don't have to decide now, anyway,' said Zainab.

'Yeah, it doesn't have to be a thing,' said Emilia, slinging her arm around Laurie.

'Thanks.' Laurie wanted to rush off to the loos to silently scream inside a cubicle or burst into tears.

But then Zoe said, 'Don't look now, but . . .'

Everyone's heads swung around.

Charley and Ben Kalu were standing together in the corner of the field, heaping fuel on the dating-rumour fire. Charley was saying something, Ben was laughing. And then they looked in Laurie's direction and waved.

'She's coming over,' said Zoe.

Charley strode towards them, her hair dazzling with the light of a thousand newly born stars.

Emilia looked sweaty. 'I've left my swimming kit in my locker!'

'Swimming's not until after lunch,' said Annie reassuringly.

'If you get it now,' said Zoe sensibly, 'you'll be carrying it around with you for ages.'

'I need it!' said Emilia, and she rushed off.

Zainab looked pointedly at Laurie. 'I'll go after her.'

Annie gave Laurie's arm a squeeze and said she'd leave Laurie to it, and that she and Zoe would see her later.

Laurie felt her cheeks go hot again. She quickly fished in her pocket for a hair tie, and twisted her hair up into a ballerina bun.

As soon as Charley reached her she skipped the small talk and got straight into talking about the competition.

'So, what we've got right now is what The Disruptors call massive exposure to an engaged audience. The vlog is a success but we have to build on that and prepare for the school sale. It's this Sunday!'

Laurie nodded. 'I know.'

She'd spent all of last night helping Fern to make her costume for the march. Even though Mum and Dad could have been nicer about how the dates had clashed, she still felt awful about not going, when it meant so much to them.

She bit her lip. 'I know the school sale is important and I'll be there! But I can only stay until mid-afternoon, say three o'clock? There's a march on in town and I need to go to the last hour. So if I run the facials until then, could you—'

'What? No way are you shirking out early! This is our big chance to grab those sales and make the biggest profit we can before—'

'It's only the last hour!'

Charley put on a mocking baby-voice. 'It's only a massive competition!'

Laurie's heart flipped.

'We're so close to winning. Let's not mess up now.'

Laurie clenched her hands. 'OK, shall we meet in

the library later to talk ideas?'

'I've got to pack. I'm off on the Biology field trip tomorrow, which means I'm away for three days. It's up to you to organize everything.'

'What?' Laurie's stomach fizzed. How could Charley not have mentioned that she had a trip to go on, on the week of the actual final?

'I know! It's to Wales. We're studying the lagoons and the limestone reefs of the Menai Strait, in Anglesey. We might see seals and porpoises. Can't wait!'

'You didn't mention that! I'm not sure I can do it all by myself.'

Charley flashed her magnetic smile. 'Course you can!' She reached over to Laurie's collar and pulled Laurie's tie out over her jumper. Then she re-knotted it until it looked the same as her own. 'Just because wearing this uniform is like being in Fashion Prison doesn't mean we can't make it look a bit better.'

'Thanks,' Laurie muttered. She could easily change it back before Zainab and Emilia saw it. There was no way she could face them with a Charley Tie. Laurie looked down. *But it looks so good! I could practically be on StyleFile! Shirt, £2, and tie, £1.50, from the School Uniform Seconds box, bought by Mum at the Summer Fayre last year.*

'Sooooooo, what we need is something new. Something mind-blowingly awesome and authentic. We are not selling products, according to The Disruptors app, we need to sell a DREAM.'

Laurie gulped. 'OK.'

The idea of the school sale was to have a last big rush of sales, but the best way to do this, said The Disruptors, was to package up your product or service in an exciting way (so people would be drawn to your stall) and offer discounts, or something new to add real value.

'So, come up with a showstopper. We can't just have the products laid out on a table, we need to offer an experience.' Charley fixed her piercing eyes on Laurie. 'And whatever you do, don't screw it up.'

*

The next day, School Stories was full of the Biology field trip. There were amazing photos of gorge walking, wild swimming and studying the estuarine eco system. Of course, Charley's feed was full of selfies and she looked like she was on a fashion shoot in the land of #Seals&Sparkles. But at least she was still talking about the competition.

@StyleFile My face is taking a knocking from the sea air. I need to amp up my routine. But Skin Warrior and Toffee Pops are totally here for it. #beachbeauty #seaskin.

@StyleFile I found it SUPER hard to find a fragrance that captured my personality. And then I discovered Charisma from @Beauty in the Kitchen!

'Switch that phone off, please,' said Laurie's dad, raising his eyebrows in the rear-view mirror. 'This is family time.'

'OK.'

Laurie rested her head against the window of the car

as they bumped along the streets. Her mum was at her Women's Equality Party meeting, Radzi had his techie friends over to do a check of the microplants, and she'd gone with her dad to pick Fern up from her ukulele lesson.

'Here, look what I found,' said Laurie's dad.

He put their favourite song from *Room on the Broom* on his phone.

'Best ever song!'

Laurie did an eye roll. 'When we were toddlers!'

A minute in, though, she was singing along and couldn't believe she still knew all the words. Fern was singing like mad and swaying her arms over her head. Fern and Dad weren't worried about their personal branding. Laurie grinned at Fern – she'd missed mucking around like this.

'We're going to ride on it. Woo-hoo!'

They were still singing as their dad pulled into a parking slot and they jumped out.

'We don't need much,' he was saying. 'A few things

for tea, that's all. Bagels and soup? Pasta? What do you guys fancy?'

'For whatever the bin has to offer, may we be truly thankful,' said Fern theatrically, with her hands together.

Bins?

Laurie instantly felt panicky.

'And we'll get a pudding too,' said her dad.

'Yass!' said Fern.

'No!' said Laurie loudly. 'I thought you said we were on our way home for dinner? I can't do this! Not now I'm so close to getting to the final of The Disruptors. Not now I'm on a team with—'

'It's just that we've not got much in,' said Dad, 'and I thought, well, I've never done one of these bin dives, and it would be so fun with you two—'

'I thought we'd stopped all this until Saturday night. Mum said the supermarkets had put some defensive messages on social media.'

'That's because it's bad publicity for them. Like your mum said, we've got them on the run. Getting stuff from the bin is completely fine.'

'Let's go home. We've got oats in the cupboards, let's have a bowl of porridge or cereal or, I don't know, something fresh.'

'This is fresh!' Her dad laughed. 'The stuff in the bin was on the shelves about ten minutes ago. It's a hundred per cent as fresh as it was then. It's moved location, that's all.'

'Yeah, to aisle *bin*,' said Fern, jumping up. 'Geddit?'

'We could go out for dinner,' said Laurie's dad with a shrug. 'There's a pizza place near here. According to the Garbage Chef, a quarter of Margheritas never get finished . . .'

'Is that meant to be funny?' said Laurie, crossly. 'After you got chucked out of . . .'

But arguing only made things worse and kept them in the danger zone for longer. She just had to get to the bins and back before anyone saw them. She could do this.

Laurie ran over to the bins, opened the first one and shrieked with surprise.

Was it a dream? A mirage? Laurie wondered if she was seeing straight. Instead of a load of salad, bread and biscuits, the entire bin was *packed with chocolate spread*. Hundreds of jars. Hundreds! Sealed. Labelled. And with a best-before date of . . .

Next week.

Laurie's heart thumped. It hadn't even gone off!

Fern and Dad came running over.

'What is it?'

'Are you OK?'

They peered into the bin.

'Oh! My! Gosh!' Fern pulled out a jar.

Laurie's dad's mouth was gaping open. 'I think that's pudding sorted.'

'There's so much!' said Laurie, without thinking. 'We've got to share it somehow. There's too much to take just for us.'

'But we can take *some* of it for us, can't we?' said Fern anxiously.

'Of course,' said Laurie's dad. Your mum's right,

once you start to think about food waste, you see it everywhere.'

He bent into the bin and handed jars over to Fern, who piled them up in the corner. 'And yes, Lau, let's find a way to share it.'

'Oi!' shouted a voice behind them.

'Aargh!' Fern dropped a jar of chocolate spread on the ground. It smashed.

A woman had come to the door near the back, beside the bins. A security light had snapped on and it framed her body and face in darkness, like a silhouette in a cartoon.

Laurie's dad shouted, 'No mess!'

'No mess!' was what her mum had told them to say if a member of staff ever approached. According to what she had read online, it was the bin divers' go-to line for heading off conflict.

The woman was marching over.

'Remember, girls. Most employees feel bad about this. Look, they've put this in boxes, in a clean bin, not in with loads of messy rubbish—'

'This isn't good, Dad!' said Fern. She looked frightened.

Laurie's heart was banging so hard she could hear the blood beating in her ears. She had a sudden vision of her dad in prison. Behind bars.

Laurie squeezed Fern's hand. She forced herself to smile. 'Don't worry, Ferny. This is going to be totally fine.'

Just as the woman looked as if she were about to shout again, she screwed her eyes up. 'Ed? Is that you?' she said at last. 'Edward Larksie!'

Laurie let out a slow, deep breath, near sick with relief as she listened to the conversation. It turned out that her dad had once helped Mary when she'd had problems with her job. His trade union had done the legal work for her and they'd won the case.

'Listen, that bin gets emptied about now each night,' Mary said. 'I don't like it any more than you do. So take what you like, because in a few minutes the waste disposal lot will pick it up and everything will be destroyed.'

They worked faster than they'd ever worked, passing

the jars to each other and running to the car, with three or four in their arms at a time.

'Enough,' said Laurie's dad, after a couple of minutes. 'This isn't worth risking anyone's job. Mary and the people she works with could get into trouble if anyone catches us in the bins.'

They jumped back into the car and sped off, talking about chocolate sandwiches, chocolate pancakes, chocolate and tahini biscuits, chocolate ice-cream toppings and milkshakes, and chocolate dips for strawberries and frozen bananas.

'Plus, just actual chocolate spread!' Fern unscrewed a top and stuck her hand right in, like she was Pooh Bear with a jar of honey.

'Try not to be sick,' said Laurie's dad.

'We can do lots of chocolatey snacks for the March for Climate!' said Fern. 'I've made up a brand, Lau, and designed a logo. Mum said we could print it off and put it on the snacks to make them look really good.'

'That's so cool.' Laurie smiled. 'I can't wait to do that.'

'It's called Garbage Gourmet,' said Fern. Her voice was thick with chocolate.

'Garbage Gourmet? I love it,' said Dad, thumping his hands on the steering wheel.

Laurie looked into the back of the car. She still had her head torch on and the light bobbed and shone off the jars, like dancing fireflies.

'This is the most awesome thing ever,' said Laurie, her eyes shining.

'We lucked out with Mary,' said her dad, who was in as high spirits as the others. 'Thought we were in for it back there.'

Fern reached across and hugged Laurie. She was sticky, but Laurie didn't mind.

Chocolate, chocolate, chocolate.

Suddenly Laurie had an idea. This was is it! They could do chocolate not only for the march but for the showstopper! They could have a chocolate spa! Laurie could make a pile of chocolate products. She could practically smell the thick, luscious cacao mixture that she'd . . .

She really *could* smell it. Fern's face was covered in chocolate spread and she was clutching her stomach . . .

'Stop the car,' wailed Fern.

CHAPTER SEVENTEEN

Laurie looked at the selfie that Charley had posted on School Stories. She was lying on her bed and the camera was held at a side angle, catching the shine of her lip gloss. On one side of her hair, there was a braided flower – Charley had twisted, wound and pinned the side of her hair into the shape of a rose.

The sun was falling through the open door and Charley had propped herself up on pillows, so she was caught looking effortlessly beautiful in a golden halo of light.

@StyleFile Just rolled out of bed. #Seals&Sparkles.

Hopefully that meant that she wouldn't mind Laurie calling early in the morning. Charley had said to run everything past her for the Event.

'A chocolate spa? It's a yes from me,' said Charley immediately, when Laurie explained her idea.

'We can sell any of the other products we still have left,' said Laurie, 'the Skin Warrior, Charisma and Toffee Pops. But a new chocolate face mask will be really fun for everyone to try!'

'Go for it.'

Charley spun her phone around so that Laurie could see the bunk beds in the dormitory at the school residential centre.

'Where is everyone?'

'No idea.' Charley yawned, and stretched her arms over her head. 'Wow, can't believe it's morning already.'

'OK, well, we could make a rich, thick cacao face mask. I've got all the ingredients at home, apart from coconut oil.'

'My mum has some of that. I'll get it for us.'

'Really? Can you ask her now so I know we can definitely do it?'

'She's always busy, she won't answer,' said Charley. She did a little flick of her hair. 'It's not like she'll notice if I take it, anyway.'

'OK,' said Laurie. Charley had sounded sad just then, but Laurie didn't really know what to say. She was so unpredictable that if Laurie offered sympathy, she was likely to dismiss her or make her feel silly.

'And it'll save your mum from having to root through a load of bins! I can't imagine you often find coconut oil on your little supermarket trips.'

Laurie's face flushed. 'Charley!'

Charley sat up and swung her legs over the side of the bed. 'Calm down, calm down, I'm only joking!' She switched to a more businesslike tone. 'And we're only doing facials.'

'No foot massages. No bare backs.'

'Especially not as some teachers might come.'

Charley put her hands up to her face. 'Visions! Visions! If we've got everything we need, we're looking at a hundred per cent profit. I'll get going on the social media. This is a critical time in the competition. We can't afford any more mistakes, like that row you caused with T-Dates.'

'I don't think that was my—'

'There's no issue more important than my – sorry – *our* image on social—'

'There you are!' Mrs Fitzpatrick, one of the teachers, strode into the dormitory. 'What on earth are you up to? Everyone else has already completed the worksheets on the plant life on the Skerries.'

Charley did a big yawn. 'Just woken up . . .'

'Just woken up? Charley Keating-Sloss! You've spent over an hour in the bathroom this morning. I saw you with my own eyes. The others are already on the minibus. You've got two minutes to join us!'

Charley's face disappeared from Laurie's screen.

C.H.O.C.O.L.A.T.E. Laurie could think of nothing else. Melted chocolate, cacao powder, chocolate flakes, smooth, creamy chocolate sauce . . . She knew she wanted to make a face mask with it but was struggling with the recipe. It was already the Wednesday of the final week of the competition, and it didn't help that Charley was already posting stuff about it.

> **@StyleFile** Fan of chocolate? Now you can use it on your face! The Chocolate Spa = an indulgent facial. Bouncy, hydrated skin is always in. #FTW.

To help out, Emilia and Zainab had suggested they go to the cafe and give the latest version of Laurie's chocolate face mask a go, while drinking chocolate frappés. Laurie was grateful her friends had asked her. She felt like she hadn't seen them for ages and she hoped they'd have fun hanging out together.

The others were in the queue, after the usual conversation about tap water, and Laurie plonked herself down at a free table.

Someone had left half a piece of millionaire's shortbread on a plate on the table. Laurie's stomach rumbled. *It was true what Mum said*, she thought. *Once you know about discarded food, you start noticing it everywhere – especially when you're tired and hungry.*

Zainab had bought one super-large chocolate frappé and three paper straws. They were passing it between them as Laurie applied the face mask on to Zainab and Emilia. But in the heat, the mixture of cacao powder and mashed bananas kept sliding straight off.

'Sorry!' said Laurie. She dunked her napkin in her water and dabbed at their shirts. 'I hope I haven't ruined your tops!'

'It smells good, though.' Emilia smiled.

'Thanks,' said Laurie. Her hands unconsciously touched her tie. She'd loved the way Charley had tied it for her so much that she hadn't wanted to undo it. Laurie had just loosened it each morning and put it on again. But now she felt self-conscious about it. Had she imagined the look that passed between Zainab and Emilia just then? Laurie wasn't sure. She felt a jolt of worry – all of these looks seemed to be aimed at Laurie, and Emilia and Zainab seemed closer than ever.

'A blob of the chocolate face mask fell off Emilia's cheeks and narrowly missed falling into the chocolate frappé. 'At least it's edible!' Emilia laughed.

'Might be easier if we could lie down, like a proper facial. We could always go to yours, Laurie?' Zainab said.

'Yes!' said Emilia. 'It'll be fun!'

'And we don't mind catching the bus,' said Zainab. 'In fact, we love the sound of your journey.'

'Honestly, it's a nightmare,' said Laurie. 'Takes ages.'

Emilia and Zainab exchanged another look – this time it was annoyed.

Before Laurie could change the subject, Charley's friends Orla and Elise came up close to their table. They were laughing behind their hands. Seconds later, Laurie's phone buzzed.

> **@StyleFile** This new chocolate face mask? It had better not be the stuff you're putting on your friends' faces right now!

> **@BeautyintheKitchen** Why?

> **@StyleFile** Orla and Elise say it looks like baby food! Hardly the premium, sophisticated showstopper we're looking for, Laurie!

Laurie flushed. She looked at her friends. They looked like toddlers who had covered their faces in a gooey chocolate pudding.

> **@StyleFile** Orla says it looks like you're starting a #FoulFaceChallenge.

'Wash it off, Em!' said Laurie.

'Why?'

Laurie's hands were shaking as she swiped her phone. 'Charley's seen it,' she said, feeling her throat get tight and sore. 'And she says it has to come off immediately!'

Zainab pulled a face. 'So what?' she said loyally. 'I like

it, and it's on my face, not Charley's.'

'I've got to let her know that you've got rid of it!' Laurie felt a wave of nausea. 'Charley says it doesn't look premium, so this isn't a good promotion for our product!'

'Premium!' Zainab snorted so loudly that blobs of the face mask blew off.

Laurie's phone buzzed.

'Leave it,' said Emilia.

Laurie felt a jolt of shock. Emilia sounded sharper than Laurie had ever heard her. But worse than that, she saw that both of her friends looked hurt and confused. There was an awkward moment of silence while Emilia sipped some frappé, and Zainab discreetly tried to wipe a drip of face mask from her chin.

Then Laurie's phone buzzed again.

Emilia stared at it. 'You said you'd come to the cafe with us, not sit here on your phone to her!'

'And I have!'

'And we couldn't believe it when you actually said you'd

come,' said Zainab, flashing a look of understanding to Emilia. 'Because you've not been hanging out with us for ages!'

Emilia raised her eyebrows. 'It is kind of hurtful, Laurie.'

'Hang on! You two have been going off as well.' Laurie felt fizzes of panic. Her thoughts spiralled off on a whizz of hurt from Emilia and Zainab eating pizzas together, leaving her out of the celebratory hug when Ned agreed to serenade Ben Kalu, and all those little BFF looks that passed between them.

Orla and Elise were approaching the table. Orla coughed. 'Charley says . . .'

Zainab grabbed her coat from the back of the chair. 'Charley says! Charley says!' She sounded furious.

Orla and Elise exchanged an amused look as they left the cafe.

Laurie's stomach twisted. 'Sit down, Zain! We can sort this out.'

'I'm not sure we can.'

'I think Charley's trying to call you,' Emilia said sarcastically.

Laurie's phone was vibrating so hard it was moving across the table. She didn't want to pick it up. The last person she wanted to talk to right now was Charley. Panic was rising inside her. If she didn't pick up, Charley was capable of being a lot meaner to her than Emilia or Zainab.

She could imagine Charley screaming, and telling everyone she was Bin Girl. And if they lost the competition, then all of this, thought Laurie, would have been a total waste, and Charley would never let her forget it.

Laurie picked up her phone. 'Give me two seconds to talk to her,' she pleaded. 'That's all I need!'

Zainab grabbed a napkin and wiped her face, and then Emilia did the same, and in that movement, Laurie could see her friendship with them falling apart. As she answered Charley's call, Emilia and Zainab stalked out of the cafe, leaving her all alone.

Chapter Eighteen

'What's the matter, Lau? I can tell you're not asleep.' Fern was pushing the mattress of Laurie's top bunk with her feet. She put on a funny voice. 'A problem shared, *as they say* . . .'

'Is a problem doubled. There's no reason why you should be troubled with this too, Fern.'

'Is a problem halved!' Fern swung herself up to the top bunk. 'At least tell me the *theme* of the trouble.' She got in at the end of Laurie's bed and wrapped a generous amount of the duvet around her.

Laurie looked at Fern, with her big eyes, and little button nose sprinkled with freckles. Fern had been brilliant the way she'd put up with her recently, but she wouldn't even have known where to start telling Fern about what she was feeling now.

Laurie had been going through the Zainab and Emilia cafe incident in her head, trying to see it through their eyes – and it looked bad. Really bad. And Charley had yelled at her down the phone, saying that by the time she was back from Anglesey, Laurie had better have upped her game. But there was no one better than Fern to talk to about home-made beauty recipes.

'I can't get the chocolate facial right. It's either too gloopy or too thick.'

'Hang on.' Fern jumped down, flicked the LEDs up a notch and reappeared with a jar of chocolate spread. She applied a blob of it on Laurie's wrist, like it was an essential oil. 'Our biggest successes have been beauty products that we want to eat . . .'

'Like the strawberry jelly perfume.'

'And the blood orange bath fizz! So close your eyes.'

Laurie lay back on her pillow.

Fern put on a floaty, cosmic voice, as if she were guiding a meditation. 'Relax your physical body and become at one with the chocolate spread. Breathe in the smell, let the sensation flow all the way into your stomach . . .'

Laurie shut her eyes. *This is ridiculous*, she thought. *Though, also, lovely and calming.*

'Now think of the nicest thing we've ever eaten that had lots of chocolate in it . . .'

Suddenly Laurie knew exactly how to make the face mask.

'You're a real star, do you know that?' Laurie gave her sister a hug as she bound into the kitchen the next morning, which was tricky because Fern was lying on the kitchen table, her face covered with peaks of chocolate aquafaba.

'That's OK! Can I talk to you about Alex and Neisha?'

'Of course.'

Though I'm the last person you should ask for friendship advice, thought Laurie. The lump in her throat was threatening to rise again as she thought about yesterday's fight.

Laurie spread peaks of aquafaba on to Fern's cheeks. 'Here goes.'

Marika, the founder of the RRFM, had given Laurie's mum her own special chocolate meringue pie recipe. The meringue was made by whipping aquafaba – the thick water that chickpeas come in – and baking it at a very low temperature. And the chocolate ganache was melted dark chocolate, coconut oil and oat cream.

Laurie was going to make a huge pie – with the real chocolate spread – for the others to give away for free at the March 4 Climate. And she was using the recipe as inspiration for the face mask, by making a thick ganache with cacao powder and coconut oil. As long as Charley got her the coconut oil in time, it should still work.

'First break was OK. I played tag with Ellie Parker and Olly Headley, and that was a laugh. But on second break, after we'd had our sandwiches, Alex and Neisha said that I couldn't play with them because I don't have any lip balms.'

Laurie was confused. 'But you have got lip balms!'

She pointed to the fridge. 'Fern, there's loads of them in there. We made the Turkish Delight ones, remember? Take some in so you can play!'

'Neisha said mine don't count because they're home-made,' said Fern.

Laurie thumped the bowl of aquafaba down on the table.

'You know the little twisty ones that look like lipsticks?' said Fern. 'They said I needed those. Neisha's got some fruity ones, and Alex has got a bubblegum-flavoured one. They were playing Make-Up Counters so they said it's nothing personal, but because I don't have any *proper* lip balms . . .'

Laurie's eyes went shiny with tears. She understood her parent's reasoning about why you shouldn't buy things to fit in with friends, but there was also a point at school where you needed some bought stuff. And she felt that Fern was at that point.

'They said there was no way for me to play the game.'

It was the sort of thing that Charley would say. But Fern

shouldn't have to put up with that! *Once this competition is over*, thought Laurie, *instead of buying myself some hot chocolate at the cafe, I'm going to buy Fern some of those twisty little lip balms. In every flavour.*

'So what did you do?'

'I said I would never buy one of those lip balms,' said Fern furiously. 'Even if my lips cracked apart like an Easter egg.'

'What?'

Fern stood up. 'I told them how the microplastics in those lip balms are turning our rivers and seas into a massive plastic soup. And that the plants in the oceans are dying and that the poor whales and seals and dolphins are eating all of the pollution and getting sick!'

The chickpea mixture was dripping off Fern's cheeks. 'I said that the nasty chemicals in the lip balms aren't good for them either, and that companies only sell planet-destroying, unhealthy, over-priced products so they can get rich!'

'Wow,' said Laurie.

'Haven't finished.'

'Sorry.'

Fern went on. 'And I said that if playing Make-Up Counters with them meant I had to help to kill our precious world, then they could forget it!'

'You're awesome, Fern.' Laurie grabbed a towel, splashed on some cold camomile tea and wiped Fern's face. *But you don't half make life harder for yourself.*

'Were they OK with you afterwards?'

Fern nodded. 'I mean, not great or anything, but Neisha did say later that she liked my lip balms really, and when I told her that the girls at Silverdale High are going mad for them, she was, like, "Oh whoa, so they *are* real".'

Laurie put her arm around Fern.

'And she asked if she could have one. She wants Turkish Delight flavour.' Fern furrowed her eyebrows. 'Shall we give her one?'

'No.'

Just then, Radzi came into the kitchen. 'What's all this,

are you dressing up as a meringue, Fern?'

'No! This is my product for the school sale,' Laurie said. 'I've made the hazelnut chocolate pavlova for you guys to take to the march, and I've adapted the chocolate ganache layer into a face mask.'

'Can you do me next?'

'Course!' Laurie grinned.

'It's perfect,' said Fern.

Laurie took a photo of the chocolate face mask and sent it to Charley.

> **@StyleFile** I have finally found THE facial of my dreams. And I'm never going back. #Authenticbeauty #FTW.

The next day, Laurie was on her way from Maths to Spanish. Zainab and Emilia were slightly ahead of her. Even though they were in a higher Maths set than Laurie, the three girls usually walked together to the Maths block and Laurie said goodbye to them outside her classroom as they went into the one next door.

Laurie was trying not to let herself get upset, when suddenly Charley arrived in the corridor and hugged Laurie in front of everyone. 'We're going to absolutely smash it at the school sale! I did an offer on the chocolate facials – I gave out a fifteen-per-cent-off offer code to anyone who liked one of my posts about the facial. And believe me, the response was *immense*.'

There was a sudden movement in Laurie's chest like a flock of birds swooping up into the sky. The competition was so nearly over. She glanced over at Zainab and Emilia, who looked like they were walking even faster. Laurie bit her lip.

'Is the chocolate facial ready to go?' Charley asked.

'Nearly. But I've run out of coconut oil. So I'm not sure where to get it, unless we release some of the money we've made so far and buy some oil?'

'No.' Charley shook her head. 'Let's keep on getting things for free because it seriously ups our profits when we don't have to use the money we're making on anything else. Leave it to me. I told you, I'll get the coconut oil.'

'Cool,' said Laurie as the bell rang for the next lesson. She wanted to add that some coconut products were dodgy and they had be careful, but a load of other girls arrived and Charley disappeared into the crowd.

@TheDisruptors It's nearly time for the school sale tomorrow, folks! #BePrepared.

@StyleFile Coconut oil. Sorted.

@BeautyintheKitchen Great. What's the brand, btw?

Charley sent her a photo of the jar, showing the label.

Oh no!

Laurie's heart thumped. She was going to have to say something. She felt bad enough about the misleading vlog for Toffee Pops, but there was a limit to what she was willing to do for this competition, for what she was willing to do for Charley, and using this sort of coconut oil absolutely hit that limit.

@BeautyintheKitchen So sorry, Charley, but we can't use that. I'm not being mean to your mum, but that's not an ethical brand.

@StyleFile What?

@BeautyintheKitchen Charley! That company uses child labour to get the coconuts. Honestly! I watched a whole documentary on it.

Laurie felt ill when she thought of the heart-breaking scenes on the documentary, of small children having to climb dangerously fast to collect the coconuts. Her stomach turned. Surely Charley would realize they couldn't support a company that did that?

@StyleFile Well, it's not like my mum knew that!

@BeautyintheKitchen I'm not saying she did! This isn't about your mum! But it trains monkeys to collect the coconuts too. They treat them really badly, chaining them to handlers and . . .

@StyleFile OK. AGREED. I get it. But Mum's bought the jars. We can't do anything about that now. We can't save the monkeys, but we can save the Chocolate Spa #FTW.

@StyleFile is typing . . .

@StyleFile Once you've mixed the stuff with cacao, who's going to see the branding?

@BeautyintheKitchen That's not the point, though. Lots of people know about how unethical the coconut industry can be. One of the girls at school might ask if it's been responsibly sourced.

Because Laurie was in the kitchen while she was messaging Charley – sitting on the kitchen counter, next to her mum, who was making tea – it didn't seem as real as it did at school. It was easier to stick up for herself on School Stories than it was when she was face to face with Charley.

Laurie's mum was making 'James and the Giant (Baked) Peaches' and Fern was sitting on the floor, finishing her March 4 Climate 'ugly carrot' costume for the following day.

The costume was Laurie's dad's orange puffer jacket, which came to below Fern's knees, and she was wearing it with orange tights and a green hat covered with carrot top leaves (made out of paper). The idea was to highlight how many misshapen 'ugly' carrots are thrown away, even though they're edible.

'That's really . . . eye-catching.'

'I'm putting some funny lumps in the sleeves of the jacket,' said Fern. 'To make it look bumpy and a weird shape. I mean, these carrots taste the same as the straight, perfect ones. I can't believe there are piles of them that get chucked.'

Laurie's mum stepped over the green leaves that Fern was painting and grabbed a clove of garlic. 'I'm still so disappointed that your spa day is the same day as March for Climate,' she was saying.

Laurie looked up from her phone. 'It's not my fault!'

Her mum raised her eyebrows. 'Didn't say it was anyone's fault, Laurie, it's one of those things. But I'd love to be there for you.'

'It's OK,' said Laurie. 'Thanks for buying a ticket, anyway.'

There was a tiny sad feeling inside her that said her mum had been there for her for every single thing she'd ever done at primary school, from school plays to sports days. But the last thing she wanted was for her mum to meet Charley again. And Emilia and Zainab probably wouldn't *want* to meet her now . . .

'Remember, I'm going to come to the end of the march, after the spa's finished,' said Laurie.

Laurie's mum gave her an oniony pat.

@StyleFile But who would ever know?

Laurie tapped out a message.

@BeautyintheKitchen Us. We'll know.

@StyleFile But that doesn't matter, does it?

@BeautyintheKitchen I think it does!

'Maybe we could do a mini facial at home, after the climate change march?' Laurie's mum looked hopeful. 'I love the sound of it.'

'You're on.'

@BeautyintheKitchen I think this stuff matters.

@StyleFile Yeah, but I DON'T THINK IT DOES.

Laurie couldn't think what to say next. Charley was so used to getting her own way that it was actually really hard to say no to her. Because she sort of didn't let you.

The thing is, though, this time it is *no*, thought Laurie. She refused to use that coconut oil. All she needed to say was . . .

Laurie's phone buzzed.

@StyleFile Do you want to win, or not?

Chapter Nineteen

Laurie woke up early on Sunday morning, leaped out of bed, and ran downstairs to the kitchen. She threw on an apron. No way was she going to use the coconut oil from Charley, so she needed to tweak the recipe so it didn't need coconut oil. But it did have to have coconut in it because of all the descriptions of the treatment they'd posted on School Stories about the creamy, tropical smell.

In the end, Laurie found some powdered coconut – light as icing sugar, not the desiccated stuff – and she mashed it into the olive oil in the fridge. Because it was cold, mixing in the coconut powder worked really well.

'Laurie!' Her dad came into the kitchen. 'Good. You're already awake. We should have some breakfast.'

He stuck some bread in the toaster for them both

and Laurie boxed everything up. She ran upstairs to scramble into her best jeans and trainers. By the time she was ready, her dad was waiting for her in the hallway. And Fern, her mum and Radzi were there too.

'I'm going to drop Lau off at school,' her dad said, giving her some toast to eat in the car. 'Then I'll be back, and we'll go into town.'

Laurie's mum and Fern both gave Laurie a hug.

She was feeling even more nervous now, and massively wishing she was off to the march instead. 'Good luck. I hope you have fun and that everyone likes the chocolate meringue pie.'

'They'll love it!' said Fern. 'We've got bagels and baguettes from the bins, too, so there's loads to hand out.' She gave Laurie a paper bag with a sticker on it saying *Garbage Gourmet*. 'Made you a packed lunch.'

'Thanks, Fern!' Laurie kissed her cheek.

'That reminds me,' said Radzi. He disappeared back upstairs to his bedroom, and then came back with a box of chocolates. 'I won these, for a Science challenge at uni,' he said. 'Thought you might want them for your chocolate spa.'

Then everyone was hugging her and saying good luck, and Laurie was feeling twists of guilt at how supportive and lovely they were being, even though she knew they were still disappointed at her choices. She told herself to stay positive as she and her dad drove to school. *They'll be fine at the march, and I'm ready for the school sale. I'm packed, I'm prepped, I'm on my way.*

'Right then, everyone!' Mrs Kapoor clapped her hands together. She was wearing jeans and a T-shirt instead of her usual wide-leg trouser suit. 'Welcome to our school sale. Our students have worked incredibly hard.' She looked around the crowded school hall, full of family and friends and pupils.

'There are so many wonderful businesses, from art to stationery, homeware to food . . . we've got pancakes, dating services, coding masterclasses, a chocolate spa, there are decorations, jewellery, woodwork . . .'

Whenever Mrs Kapoor mentioned a business, the team would wave and shout. The jogging-bottoms lot were hopping up and down on the spot, T-Dates were dressed in red, with love-heart stickers on their faces, Emilia and Zainab had birthday balloons tied to their doggy biscuit bags . . .

Mrs Kapoor carried on for a minute, talking about what The Disruptors had taught the pupils, then said: 'And I'm delighted to announce that Silverdale High has made it to the final – we're one of two local schools that may be crowned the overall winner . . .'

There was a spontaneous round of applause.

'Which means that Avril Delamere will be coming to our assembly on Monday morning – Amy is going to the other school – and they've asked the winning team from our school to make a short presentation to them about the real value of their business.'

The presentation only needed to be a few minutes long, Mrs Kapoor explained, but it would help the Delamere sisters decide on which school would win – and be awarded the 4D printer.

'So while you should all already be proud of yourselves, there's even more at stake today. So good luck, everyone!'

'So what kind of leg-up does chocolate have on regular facials?' asked Lexi, the editor of the school magazine. 'BTW, I'm capturing the vibe by talking to the front-runners.'

Charley grinned. 'Cacao isn't incorporated into the facial treatment *just because*,' she said, in her confident, polished way. 'It's packed with antioxidants, which can help your face look healthier, fresher and cleaner.'

She ran Lexi through the treatment, both of them completely ignoring Laurie, who was rushing around setting everything up. 'Awesome!' Lexi panned her camera around. She took in the armchair that Laurie had carried from the staff room and draped with silvery material, and the chocolate meringue pie facial on the table beside it. (Lexi zoomed in on that.) It was next to a pile of flannels, a bowl of warm water, some cucumber glow tonic, a jug of cold water with sliced strawberries and mint leaves, and Radzi's box of chocolates.

'Naturally, the grand finale of the treatment is eating chocolate, as well as wearing it!' said Charley.

Lexi was eyeing up the chocolates. Charley offered her one, and took one herself. Laurie was about to stop her when Abigail Sutton, a girl from Year 8, and her mum came over and asked for a facial. Lexi dashed off to film someone else, and Laurie offered Abigail and her mum a glass of strawberry and mint water.

'Charley, do you want to start with the cucumber glow tonic to ensure Abigail's face is cleansed?'

Charley pulled a face. 'I was going to get some blueberry pancakes.' She pointed to a stand in the far corner that had an electric hob. There were lots of squeals as pancakes were flipped over.

'Can't you do that in a sec?' said Laurie, feeling the tension rising even more. Charley hadn't been too sniffy about Laurie not using her mum's coconut oil, which

Laurie was pleased about, but she hadn't particularly wanted to see her after their disagreement the night before. Things had gone so far from the Beauty in the Kitchen products she loved making with Fern – the fun, affordable, home-made ranges – that it almost didn't feel real.

But once she saw how Charley was dressed, she had thought she might do some work – she was in a white coat, like she worked in a real beauty spa.

She did her tinkly laugh. 'I've taken care of our media interview, as well as doing all our promos on social!' She sighed deeply, in a way that made Laurie feel small, whiny and pathetic. 'Surely you can take care of the facials?'

Laurie dug her nails into her palms. 'Fine.'

She got a bottle of cucumber tonic, wiped it over Abigail's cheeks with a cotton pad, and the day began.

It was unbelievably hectic. Laurie knew that was a good thing for them, but by the afternoon her feet were aching from standing up and she was feeling pretty stressed, worrying about how things were going for the others at the march.

She had no time to get a drink, let alone wander around the hall, but anyone who came for a facial filled her in. She heard how Ned had been paid to sing a proposal of marriage from Rizwana's dad to her mum ('If that's not a product that makes the world a better place, I don't know what is!' said Lexi, on School Stories); that the organic pancake stall had sold out; and that Mrs Kapoor had been T-Dated with Mr Henderson, the Geography teacher.

Laurie had never worked so hard on anything in her life. But if she could stay ahead and keep going, there would be a real chance of winning the school competition. And then – she hardly dared to think about it – if they won that, they would get to do the presentation to Avril Delamere and might be crowned the overall winners of The Disruptors . . .

She glanced over at Charley, who was standing

nearby, going on to her friends Orla and Elise about how much she wanted to meet the Delamere sisters.

'I've got their glittery rainbow trainers,' Charley said. 'Plus, the aquamarine striped pair and the ones with tangerine sequins, but I got them last summer, so I hardly wear them now.'

'And you've got the navy and pink-star pair,' said Elise.

Charley laughed. 'Oh yeah.'

Laurie felt a knot of tension growing in her stomach.

Keep it together, Lau, she told herself. *This is about being Beauty Girl, not Bin Girl*. She was in with a real chance of winning the competition and it would be LIFE-CHANGING! *And after today*, she told herself, *I'll never have to speak to Charley Keating-Sloss ever again. Come on, Lau, you can do this*.

And she did. Until the late afternoon, when her phone started ringing.

Laurie was in the middle of a facial – she was holding the chocolate meringue pie in one hand, and applying the ganache layer of it to Annie's face with the other.

But she had a second before she had to wipe Annie's cheeks so she could check her phone. There were three missed calls from Radzi. Weird.

She tried to call him back but it went straight to voicemail. So she tried to call her mum's phone, and then her dad's, but there was no answer from them either. Laurie got a panicky feeling that something was badly wrong.

And then she saw a list of notifications on the news app. She'd set it to update her with anything #March4Climate so that she could keep up to date with the others. But until now, she hadn't had time to check.

A headline popped up.

12.25 p.m.: Food Waste Activists Chain Themselves to Supermarket Bins.

The pie nearly slipped out of Laurie's hand.

'What are you doing?' called Charley. She was at the next stall, having her hair sprayed with ombre pink strands. 'Don't drop that thing!'

Laurie's face flushed pink with panic. 'I think

something's happening at the march. I think I need go and see what . . .'

Her phone went off again. *14.42 p.m.: Arrests made at the March 4 Climate.*

Oh. My . . .

No! Her parents wouldn't have been arrested, would they? They wouldn't go that far for discarded Hobnobs and hummus? But Laurie was worried that they might. They were so determined, and they'd been looking forward to the march for weeks, and . . .

There was another buzz: *Live footage! Police move in on food waste activists.*

Laurie's heart was pounding as she pressed play on the clip of the march. There was loads of background noise and a fuzzy picture. The phone the clip was filmed on was shaking, but you could see some police officers arriving, and the voiceover was saying that some people had been arrested. And it was clear that her mum and dad were among them.

But it was the corner of the screen that Laurie couldn't

take her eyes off. There was a little figure dressed as an ugly carrot in the crowd, totally alone. Laurie's heart felt like it could burst out of her body.

Fern!

Laurie thought quickly. What was the fastest way to get to town? Which bus did she need to take? When was that clip filmed? Fern could be anywhere by now. Her parents could be locked up and on their way to prison. *Help, help, help!*

Laurie's chest felt all squished, like someone was squeezing it tightly. The blood was pounding in her ears. It was getting hard to breathe.

Zainab and Emilia came rushing over.

'What is it?' asked Emilia. 'We saw you from across the hall, looking like you're about to—'

'What is it?' said Zainab.

'It's Fern! I think she might be lost. And my mum and dad have been arrested! And—'

'How do you know?' said Zainab, looking concerned.

'A local news site has posted a clip of people

being taken away by officers.'

'It might not be true,' said Emilia quickly. She put her arm around Laurie. 'It's really easy to manipulate stuff like that!'

Zainab nodded. 'Don't panic, Laurie. We'll help you find out what's going on, but like Emilia says, this could be fake news.'

But Laurie knew it wasn't. She knew no one could fake an ugly-carrot costume. There was only one person in the world who would wear a massive knitted sock attached to an orange puffer jacket . . .

'They're right, it's probably hype!' said Charley, coming over to join them. 'You don't have to run to them all the time, you know. The chances are, your sister is with your parents, and they're picking themselves a sandwich from the bins.'

'What?' Zainab turned on Charley.

'How can you say that?' spluttered Emilia.

Pictures kept flashing through Laurie's mind. Fern lost and alone. Fern being swept along the streets in a surge of people she doesn't know. Fern so frightened she was hiding somewhere, like behind her favourite Victorian kitchen display in the local museum . . .

'It's losing the competition you should be worried about.' Charley added.

And that was the moment when Laurie had had enough.

The chocolate hazelnut meringue pie in her hands wobbled. *I need to get to Fern*, she thought, *I need to get out of here.*

Her mum and dad had been arrested. Fern was lost and alone.

Charley stared straight at her. 'We've only got half an hour left of the sale, and then Mrs Kapoor is going to announce who's won the school part of the competition!'

'As if that matters!' yelled Laurie.

'If you walk out now, our chances of winning could be over!'

'Don't you get it? *I don't care!*' And, in a massive burst of emotion, all the stress of the last three weeks exploded inside Laurie. 'You're so *selfish*. I've been doing all of this on my own, putting up with your horrible comments about me and my family for weeks. If you can't see that Fern is a thousand million times more important than being the winner, well, that's your problem!' Her arms flew up in panic. 'But it's not mine!' And somehow, the pie shot out of her hands.

And landed on Charley's face.

Without daring to look behind her, Laurie ran out of school.

CHAPTER TWENTY

Laurie kept on running and running until she got to the bus stop, and then after a few stops the roads were blocked because of the demonstration. She had to carry on running all the way from the outskirts of town.

On her way, she put her head through every shop door, yelling 'Have you seen my sister?' describing what Fern was wearing and how tall she was.

No one had seen Fern, and Laurie ran so quickly, she eventually doubled over with a stitch. Twice she'd had to stop and lean against a wall to steady herself. She held her chest to stop the pain and whispered to herself, 'Please let me find her.' She felt so distraught she thought she might break into pieces. But she kept on looking. And Laurie knew she wouldn't stop searching until she found Fern, even if this was the last thing she ever did.

Finally, when she'd raced the length and breadth of town, darting in and out of protesters, and weaving her way through all the diverted routes, she decided to check at the police station. It seemed like a long shot for Fern to have got all the way there from the supermarket, but if Fern had seen their parents being taken there, there was a chance she'd have gone after them.

Laurie yanked open the door, and the crash of relief nearly knocked her over. Fern was sitting in the waiting area. Her little neck was tilted at an angle, which made her look younger and more vulnerable than ever.

Laurie's heart flooded. There were no words big enough to describe how much she loved her sister. She threw herself down next to the girl in the oversized orange puffer jacket. She hugged her tightly, and she never, ever wanted to let go.

'I'm here, Fern. I'm here!'

'Laurie!'

Fern's face was blotchy with tears as she tried to explain what had happened. 'It was so weird and scary,

Lau. The actual march was fun.' Fern wiped her eyes and tried to smile. 'We saw Marika, by the way, and everyone loved the snacks and especially your chocolate meringue pie . . .'

Laurie shook her head. 'Forget the pie!'

Fern sniffed. 'But then some people ran around the back of the supermarket, the one that's near the waffle place, and said they were going to chain themselves to the bins until the supermarket promised to end food waste.'

Laurie bit her lip.

'And Mum went with them to see if she wanted to join in. She left me with Dad, and she said she wasn't sure she was going to do it, Laurie, because there might be a better way to get attention on the issue, but she was so brave, Lau . . .'

It was hard to work out what Fern was saying because she was crying so much. Laurie reached into her bag for a tissue, and Fern blew her nose.

'But then some other people – they weren't on the

climate change march, I don't know where they came from – arrived on the wall of the supermarket, and they jumped down on top of the bins and hurt someone's arm because they were chained to the lid. And Dad ran over to help the person who was screaming, and it was all so quick! But then the police were there . . . and they'd taken everyone beside the bins away, saying that it was private property, and some people were handcuffed and others put into police cars. And Dad thought that I was still with Radzi, but I wasn't.' Fern gulped. 'Radzi had spotted Romy in the crowd and gone over to see her while I was still safe with Dad. I was yelling and yelling to Dad and Mum, but no one could hear me.'

'So you came here all by yourself?' said Laurie. It was a long way from the supermarket to the police station. Nearly a mile, with at least three massive roads to cross. 'You're amazing!' Laurie gave Fern another huge hug.

'Radzi was here already,' said Fern. 'He'd run here to try and find Mum and Dad when he heard there'd been arrests, but it was me he found in the waiting room.

He asked the woman over there –' Fern pointed to the police officer on the reception desk – 'to keep an eye on me, while he helped sort things. He's in there with the police, telling them how responsible Mum and Dad usually are. And they know I'm OK now.'

Fern explained how their parents had come out of the room for a minute to see Fern with their own eyes – apparently they had insisted – before the officer had taken them back in for more details.

Laurie stood up. 'I'll find out what's happening.'

'Don't go,' whispered Fern.

Laurie's heart was pounding as the police officer checked the screen for an update on Polly and Ed Larksie.

'They'll be fine,' she whispered to Fern.

It seemed to take ages until the woman at the desk spoke. 'They're processing them now. Please don't worry.' She explained that the Larksies hadn't been properly arrested. They were making a statement about the march and would be out very soon.

And, in the end, they did come out. There was a lot of hugging and crying and a million apologies from Laurie's mum and dad. They wrapped themselves so tightly around Fern and Laurie that they looked like emperor penguins huddling together in a wild Antarctic snowstorm.

After a second or two Radzi patted their backs and suggested they treated themselves to a taxi ride home. That sounded good to Laurie. The tears that had built up in her since she'd seen those photos of the little girl in the carrot costume all alone were pouring down her cheeks, and she desperately wanted to get home.

And then Laurie's dad made things even better by saying how about they stopped at their favourite vegan Indian restaurant on the way and bought themselves a takeaway.

'Great idea,' said Laurie's mum and Fern.

Her dad laughed at Laurie's anxious face. 'Don't worry! It'll be fully paid for, Laurie!'

'Let's eat it on our laps while we watch *Doctor Who*,'

said Radzi. 'It's Monday tomorrow –' he had looped his arm through Fern's as they left the police station – 'and we can't have Neisha and Alex giving you a hard time.'

Fern nodded. 'But can we fast-forward the scary bits?'

Everyone laughed.

'Of course we can!' said Laurie, with feeling. 'Today's been scary enough.'

Chapter Twenty-One

When Laurie woke the next morning, everything came rushing back. She felt pale and shaky. It *was* true, wasn't it? Her mum and dad *had* been taken to the police station, and Fern *had* walked across town by herself, and she *had* walked out on the competition?

It was worse than that. *I. Threw. A. Pie. At. Charley. Keating. Sloss.*

And now it was Monday. The winner would have been announced yesterday and today two teams in different schools would have to give a presentation. Laurie had a sad, sick feeling in her stomach. It had seemed as if her and Charley had had a real chance to be one of those teams but . . .

Laurie felt a pain in her head and chest.

She'd blown it.

Laurie's phone was beside her pillow, but she'd switched it off the previous night. She'd messaged Emilia and Zainab to say Fern was safe, and powered it down without even waiting for their response.

She was going to try very hard to be glad for T-Dates, or whoever had won, but she didn't want to face it after the drama of yesterday. Then, when she couldn't put it off any longer, she felt in her bed for her phone.

> **@TheDisruptors** It's TODAY! Yes, people! It's presentation day! You all know who won in your own school – and huge congrats to them! But now the winners of two schools have been chosen to talk during assembly about how their business will make the world a better place. Once both judges have heard their school's presentation, they'll make a decision.

Just then, Fern came rushing into the bedroom.

'Got a surprise for you!'

Laurie's heart sank. *Not now, Fern.* She would have made Laurie a tahini smoothie, or rearranged their doll's house or something. And although Fern was very kind and thoughtful, all Laurie wanted to do was go on her phone, eat Marmite on toast, and stay in bed for the rest of her life.

'Close your eyes!' Fern climbed up to the top bunk and plonked what felt like a heavy box on to the bed. 'Ta-da!'

Laurie's mouth fell open.

It was a basket packed with Beauty in the Kitchen products. There was a strawberry face mask, wild rose and strawberry moisturizer, lemon drizzle lip scrub, camomile tea toner, and lime and peppermint bath fizz. All the recipes that Laurie and Fern had invented together. The really good stuff.

'This is unbelievable. Thank you, Fern!'

'It wasn't just me. Mum, Dad and Radzi worked on them too. We all know you've been . . . under pressure.' Fern looked sad for a moment. 'Mum and Dad are sorry they made things too hard for us yesterday. You do like the hamper, don't you?'

'Like it?' Laurie's eyes swam. 'I love it!'

'But is it good enough?'

'For what?'

'To take into school today?'

'It's better than good enough!' Laurie said. She bit her lip. 'But I didn't tell you about yesterday, because things were so . . . Fern, I really messed up. I'm out of the competition.'

Fern looked confused. 'But you can't be.'

'Why?'

'Mrs Kapoor's just called Mum and told her that you and that Charley girl won the school competition – first place! You made loads of money. It was announced at the end of the school sale, when you weren't there!'

'What?' Laurie felt a sweet, tangy rush, like she'd stuck her tongue into a bag of sherbet. She threw off her duvet.

'So you have to do a presentation today . . .'

Laurie hopped around the room, trying to get her tights on. She had one arm in her school shirt.

'. . . in front of that trainer woman, Avril, and there's a really good chance, Mrs Kapoor told Mum, that you're going to win! But you have to get the bus. Like, now!'

As she ran downstairs, Laurie was enveloped in hugs from her mum and dad and Radzi. Quickly she grabbed the hamper of products, and with her shirt untucked and her tie flying, Laurie absolutely legged it up the lane.

It was only on the bus that the news began to sink in. First place in school and either runner-up or overall winner! That was unbelievable. After the disaster of yesterday she thought she was more likely to be disqualified. She flicked her phone on. School Stories was totally lit up with excitement about the final.

She scrolled through the messages – there was a breathless thread from Lexi about Laurie throwing the pie, but only a few people had the nerve to like it – and lots of people were excited about the presentation. But Laurie was feeling nervous. She didn't know if she could do this. How could she stand up there on the stage with

Charley, after everything that had happened? Laurie wasn't even sorry she had thrown that pie. In fact, she was glad – Charley had deserved it.

And then she thought of Fern, and how brave she'd been in the carrot costume, and Laurie knew that she had to go on.

'There you are, Laurie,' said Mrs Kapoor when she arrived at school. 'Go straight to the hall, please. Best of luck!'

As Laurie nervously walked across the hall, she saw Charley sitting on the edge of the stage. Her hair was braided into a regal flower crown and dotted with real aster buds.

Turns out she was not the brand builder of my dreams, thought Laurie. Teaming up with Charley had been a massive mistake. If only she could do this whole thing again, she would choose a very different person to showcase the products on their face.

She should have chosen someone funny, zingy and honest, who truly believes in everything Beauty in the

Kitchen stands for. Someone so brave that she didn't need things like trainer-approval from the popular kids at school to feel good about herself. In other words, Fern.

'Earth to Laurie!'

Laurie came to with a jolt. The school hall was filling up for assembly. In the Year 7 row, she could see her friends. Zainab and Emilia gave her a thumbs up.

'I'm glad you found your sister,' said Charley. She swung her legs up as she and Laurie took their place on the side of the stage. 'Sorry if I didn't realize how important it was to you.'

'Thanks.' Laurie did her best to look grateful. Had that been an apology? She wasn't sure. It was a bit like saying 'Sorry you're offended' rather than 'Sorry I said something offensive', but maybe she could do the same and they could call it quits. 'And I'm glad to see you got the meringue out of your hair.'

Charley laughed lightly. 'Ha! Don't worry about this presentation, by the way. I can't wait to present to one of the Delamere sisters.' She wiggled her feet. 'Have you noticed that I've got their very latest pair of trainers?'

Laurie didn't even bother to look down. She knew what she had to do, so she just came out and said it.

'I'm going to do the presentation, Charley, because I'm the one who knows our products the best and can talk about the story behind them.'

A flash of annoyance went across Charley's face.

'To a point! But no one wants to know the products they've been slapping on their cheeks come from ingredients from the bins. So don't, you know, go back to the beginning, for goodness sake.'

'Yes they do!' said Laurie. 'And you did put down "food waste" as our way to make the world a better place, so we need to explain that. And we should anyway, because it's the whole idea behind our business.' Laurie put down the hamper of products on the table near them. 'You can show people the products, you're good at that, but this time I'm doing the talking.'

'But I'm the one with the biggest following, so . . .'

But there was no more time to argue.

'The stage is yours!' said Mrs Kapoor.

And suddenly they were on.

'The beauty industry can seem really glamourous and exciting,' said Laurie. Her voice was shaking, but she knew if she didn't start speaking straight away she wouldn't have to nerve to do this. And besides, Charley would probably cut in.

Actually, even though she wasn't speaking, everyone was staring at Charley, who was rooting through the hamper, looking at the products. But Laurie's voice was now somehow more confident, and she sounded more compelling than ever, because very soon, everyone was paying her their full attention.

'. . . But the chemicals it takes to produce cosmetics and the waste the industry produces is having a catastrophic effect on our land, our oceans and the atmosphere. So Beauty in the Kitchen was invented to not only solve blocked pores but help save the planet.'

Charley had opened some lip sugar. She rubbed it on thickly and licked her lips. 'I'm sold!'

There was a murmur of approval from the audience.

Laurie watched her. There was an undeniable power to Charley. In some ways, girls like her set the tone for the way everything in school operated. She was brainy, beautiful, on-trend. Charley knew she had clout, and she used it.

But if the only reason we win is because of the power of her money and looks, then I don't want to win at all, thought Laurie. She took a deep breath. Beauty in the Kitchen was not expensive. It was not *premium*. At its heart, it was Laurie and Fern putting yogurt on their faces. And that was for everyone.

Win or lose, Laurie knew that the competition itself had been life-changing – in some ways, the events of the last three weeks had helped her find the courage to really go for what she believed in.

'Is that the lemon drizzle lip sugar?' said Laurie.

Charley nodded.

'I got the lemons in that recipe free from the bins at our local supermarket.'

There was a ripple of uneasy laughter around the room.

Laurie's heart thumped. 'No, really! I did. The whole point of Beauty in the Kitchen is that it's different. It's a way we can use waste food that's chucked out – perfectly good stuff that's lying around in bins at supermarkets, cafes and restaurants, or even just going off in our own fruit bowls at home – and use it to give us shiny skin and glossy hair.'

Charley tapped her fingers lightly on her cheeks. 'And this isn't some kind of School Stories illusion,' she said.

Laurie held her breath.

'Our products look good in real life, as well as online.' Charley looked sincere. 'Because I'm not wearing a filter right now, am I?'

There was some light applause.

'And we wouldn't want to disguise the true story of our products either,' Charley added. 'So, we like to think of them as less Beauty in the Kitchen and more . . . Beauty and the Bin!'

There was a proper breakout of applause and some laughter.

Laurie's heart went into a spin. Beauty and the Bin! It was perfect! *If only Charley had been OK with this from the start.*

She quickly pulled herself together. 'When bananas are too ripe to even be eaten in a smoothie, they can make a fudgy hair conditioner! Squashy strawberries can cleanse your skin, and we all know the power of a supercharged tomato skin serum!'

'Don't forget Toffee Pops!' someone shouted.

Laurie grinned. 'The idea is that Beauty and the *Bin* is a fun, affordable, inclusive, plant-based way for everyone to have clearer skin! Or pink-tinged hair! You can do that with old beetroots, by the way. Works even on mine.' She lifted a molasses-coloured lock. 'So, what I'm saying is, this is an idea I believe in. Maybe it's a tiny thing, but even those can change the world, can't they?'

Laurie could barely contain her nerves as Mrs Kapoor introduced Avril from The Disruptors, who had been at the back of the hall. Laurie felt everything from tension, so far up her throat that she felt almost sick, to sparkles of excitement in her toes.

'Good morning!' said Avril, bouncing on to the stage in the funkiest trainers the world had ever seen. 'My sister Amy and I are so impressed with the standard of entries this year. Well done, everyone! But there can only be one overall winner, and . . .'

Charley grabbed Laurie's hand and squeezed it.

'We've decided that Beauty and the Bin is truly a business that could make the world a better place. So it's my great pleasure to announce that this year's winners of The Disruptors are Laurie Larksie and Charley Keating-Sloss, from right here, at Silverdale High!'

The school erupted with cheers and applause.

It felt like fireworks were going off in Laurie's brain. Mrs Kapoor looked like she had something in her eye,

Avril was cheering, and Charley had her arms up in the air, waving into the crowd and trying to whip up extra applause. She grabbed Laurie and squeezed her.

'I told you we'd storm this thing!' she yelled in her ear.

Laurie dived into her bag for her phone. People were crowding around and congratulating her. But somehow she managed to quickly message her mum to tell her the news, and to ask her to tell her dad, Fern and Radzi as soon as she could.

And then Laurie made sure she said well done to T-Dates and the personalized-stationery lot, and the team who did the coding workshops, as she ducked through everyone – people were streaming out of the glass doors and into the corridor on their way to morning lessons – to find Zainab and Emilia.

As Laurie walked, she could hear Charley giving an interview to Lexi for the school magazine. 'Life is a journey and the perfect skincare is a destination,' she was saying.

Charley looked up and held Laurie's gaze for a moment.

Laurie shook her head. She wasn't sure she'd ever quite work Charley Keating-Sloss out. She had come through for her in the presentation, though, and right now Laurie was just relieved it was all over and she could get back to her friends. As soon as she found Zainab and Emilia, they pulled her into a real three-way hug.

They pulled apart in the end and Zainab smiled. 'We should celebrate!'

'How about we go to the cafe after school tonight?' said Emilia tentatively.

Zainab gave Laurie a gentle nudge with her elbow. 'Now you've made so much money, you can buy an entire lemon drizzle cake!'

'I'm not sure I can face that place right now,' said Laurie, suddenly feeling awkward. She looked at them both. 'I am so sorry about going off like that with Charley. I can see how awful I must have looked. I guess I just got carried away with how . . . sparkly she is.'

Emilia squeezed her arm. 'It's OK. We're just glad that you found Fern and everything's worked out.'

'And we feel bad too,' said Zainab. 'We should have realized how much pressure you were under.'

They all looked over at Charley. She was taking a selfie with Lexi. 'School is wild!' she was saying. 'Life is wild . . .'

Laurie pulled her phone out. 'Here goes. I am officially deleting Charley Keating-Sloss from my contacts.' She hit the button, knowing it was the right thing to do. 'Done!'

The three of them laughed.

'But can we just talk about your presentation?' said Emilia as they left the school hall and made their way to lessons. 'Why didn't you tell us about the food waste idea?'

'It's awesome!' said Zainab. 'You really save edible food from bins and use it for beauty products?'

Laurie nodded. 'And I didn't even mention that I also use the herbs we grow on the walls at home.'

Emilia and Zainab looked confused.

'I've got an idea! Instead of the cafe, would you like to come to mine, after school?'

*

305

Laurie and her friends jumped off the bus. The journey had been such a laugh. They'd bumped into Radzi, who had got on outside the university. He'd made a huge fuss of Laurie and a big impression on Zainab and Emilia, and they were in very high spirits as they arrived at Orchard End.

'Look at that!' said Zainab.

'Wow!' said Emilia.

There was a sheet with the words *Well Done, Our Lau!*, painted by Fern, flapping about in the breeze. And Laurie's mum had hung flowers in old chickpea tins on the fence. The solar-powered Christmas lights had been strung around the windows, ready to shine the second it got dark. Laurie cringed. *What were Mum and Dad thinking?*

Laurie stared at Radzi. *Help*, she mouthed.

Radzi chuckled. 'You can't beat home!' he said warmly.

Zainab went over to the magnolia tree and looked at an illustration of a red pepper that was stuck to a branch.

Laurie smiled. Fern had obviously gone into overdrive as soon as she'd got home from school. She'd drawn little pictures of pineapples, pizzas, mangoes, cocoa beans, peppers, lemons, roses, tomatoes . . . and there were little labels: *Laurie Larksie: Winner!*

'They've done all this for you,' said Emilia. 'How totally cool!'

Laurie touched one of the decorations. It was a drawing of a Peppa Pig cake. *How totally Fern*, she thought.

And then the door banged open, and Fern came rushing out, her hair flying behind her. 'She's here!' she yelled. 'LAU'S HOME!' And Fern and Laurie's parents ran out of the house.

Laurie felt an enormous burst of happiness, like liquid sunshine pouring through her, as they threw their arms around her and held her tight.

'Thank you!' Laurie said, feeling overwhelmed. 'For everything you do for me. We could never have won without you!'

'Oh, Lau!' said her dad, ruffling her head. 'You did a really good thing today. But we're proud of you for who you are, not because you won the competition.'

Fern squeezed Laurie's arm. 'Well, I'm proud about it. I know you wanted to be the big old winner and now . . .'

Laurie's mum laughed. 'Lau was a winner long before the competition!'

Emilia coughed.

'Oh my gosh! Nearly forgot. I've brought my friends home,' Laurie whispered to her mum. 'I hope that's OK?'

Zainab and Emilia were standing smiling on the driveway.

'It's more than OK,' her mum said, in a wobbly voice.

'Wait . . . what?' said Emilia. She was staring at the leafy hallway walls.

Laurie's heart pounded.

'Laurie!' Zainab took her glasses off, wiped them, and put them back on again. 'Why didn't you tell us that your home was . . .'

'A hydroponic growing farm?' said Laurie. 'We grow food on the walls! The thing is, we couldn't get an allotment and it's . . .'

'Beautiful,' said Emilia. 'Why didn't you tell us how beautiful your home was?'

'All these plants!' said Zainab. 'This place feels so alive.'

'Do you pick things off the walls to eat?' said Emilia.

'All the time!' Laurie laughed. 'Go on,' she said to Emilia. 'Try it!'

Emilia gently twisted some basil from the hallway wall and ate it. 'That's delicious!'

Then Fern showed Laurie's friends the pineapples and gooseberries, her mum stuck a cherry crumble in the oven, and her dad did the drinks order. 'We've got peppermint tea, raspberry cordial, a rose and lavender infusion – better warn you, Fern's made that one . . .'

'So much about you makes sense now,' said Zainab, smiling. 'Your family is funny and kind, and your home smells as lovely as one of your perfumes . . .'

Emilia laughed. 'And no wonder you invent gorgeous

beauty products. You're surrounded by ingredients and inspiration!'

Laurie nodded. 'True!'

Only a few weeks ago, the idea of Laurie's friends meeting her family had sent her into panic overload. But now she didn't feel any embarrassment at all!

Well, not much, anyway. She wished her mum wasn't wearing a T-shirt that said *I'm Freegan Awesome!* and that her dad hadn't offered to make Hun-Knee sandwiches. And she could have done without Fern on Radzi's shoulders, pulling tomatoes off the ceiling and throwing them into Emilia and Zainab's mouths. But apart from *that*, it was the best feeling ever.

Suddenly Laurie's phone rang.

'Sorry to call so late. It's Amy and Avril, from The Disruptors.'

Laurie ran outside.

'We're so impressed with Beauty and the Bin!' said Amy.

'Thank you.' Laurie wriggled her bare toes into the

grass trying to contain her excitement.

'We think this idea could really take off,' said Avril. 'That its potential goes way beyond a school competition.'

'So,' added Amy, 'as we happen to know someone at your favourite beauty brand . . .'

Suddenly the words 'Laurie Larksie, entrepreneur extraordinaire' felt so close that Laurie could touch them.

'. . . we've arranged for your class to go to their labs, for the "You're the CEO Day", and see how they make sparkly bath fizz and lip scrubs, and to have a go at making some yourselves!'

'Thank you. That's brilliant!'

'While you're there, the real CEO wants to talk to you, Laurie, and hear more about your ideas for using food waste for beauty potions . . .'

Laurie's heart skipped.

'They really believe in this idea,' Amy said, 'and how it can make the world a better place, so they're keen to make it happen. And they want you to be the face of the new brand and to give you the credit for coming up with the idea. However, because you're still at school, we need to talk to your parents and teachers. But first we wanted to know what you thought about being the inspiration behind their new range.'

'It'll mean working on ideas for the products and the story behind them,' said Avril. 'They want to get your message out there, and they're hoping you'll let them launch a Beauty and the Bin range, with you behind it.'

Laurie's heart thudded. *What about Charley?* They were joint winners, after all. If it meant that she would have to work with her again, well . . . Her stomach turned. It would have to be a no. No way would she be dragged back into the world of Charley Keating-Sloss.

Laurie held her breath. 'Have you told Charley?'

'We spoke to her and her parents a few minutes ago,' said Amy.

Avril sounded like she was smiling. 'Charley told us that you *are* Beauty and the Bin. And we love the name, by the way! All she did, apparently, was put the products on her face . . .'

'In any case,' Amy said, 'she wouldn't have time. She's really pleased because now she's won the competition, her mum has asked her to help on a new PR campaign.'

'That's great!' Despite everything, Laurie was pleased for Charley. She'd send her a message later to say so.

'How about it then?'

Laurie bit her lip. 'Actually, there's one more thing, and it's very important.'

'Go on.'

'Our beauty recipes are as much about my little sister as they are about me. So it wouldn't be fair if I was the inspiration behind a new range and she wasn't. Fern really deserves this! Can she be involved too?'

'Of course she can!' Avril said.

'So what do you think?' asked Amy.

'Thank you! And YES PLEASE!' Every cell in Laurie's body was firing off showers of excitement. It was like a million pieces of popping candy were inside her, and all of them were bursting at once.

What do I think? What do I think?

I think . . .

Dream. Come. True.

@School Stories/@The Disruptors A huge well done to everyone who took part! And massive congrats go to our awesome winners: Laurie and Charley. We're proud to say the girls have given all of the money they made to charity. Every single penny! But this is only the beginning. Pop on to our blog to see students from Silverdale High on their 'You're the CEO' day, inventing the ultimate spicy gingerbread bath milk and glittery vanilla hair custard. And when you've bin there and done that, stay tuned to hear more about Laurie's adventure!

The Silverdale High
Chronicle

*** EXCITING NEWS ***

Laurie and her sister Fern are the ambassadors for a range of brilliant new Beauty and the Bin products from their favourite beauty brand! And not only that, but the girls have launched their own social media channel to show you how to make the products yourselves. Have fun watching Laurie and Fern turn kitchen leftovers into super-scrumptious face packs and lip scrubs

The End

BEAUTY AND THE BIN

Recipes

Remember to be careful if you've got any allergies, and if you're worried, test the recipes on a small patch of skin before you put it on your face.

Oaty Banana Face Pack

Ingredients

2 tablespoons of oats

¼ of a ripe banana

1 teaspoon of coconut oil

Method

Mash the banana and coconut oil with a fork and mix in the oats. Once it's a thick paste, gently massage it into your skin (cheeks, forehead and chin – it's best to skip the bit around your eyes). Leave the face pack on for a few minutes. *Top tip*: This works well if you're in the bath, as it can be quite sticky. Wash off with warm water.

Strawberry Yogurt Face Mask

Ingredients

2 or 3 squashy strawberries

1 or 2 tablespoons of yogurt

    (almond/soya/coconut/etc)

A tsp of honey (or vegan syrup) optional

Method

Mash the strawberries really well with a fork and stir in the yogurt and honey or syrup if using. Apply it to your face with your fingers. Leave it for a few minutes before rinsing it off with warm water.

Lavender Bath Bombs

This recipe makes around four small bath bombs or a jam jar of crumble.

Ingredients

60g citric acid

120g bicarbonate of soda

60g Epsom bath salts (optional)

Oil – olive oil is fine: you need around 10ml

Water – a few drops to wet your hands

Lavender essential oil – a few drops

30g Cornflour (optional)

Decorations

Dried herbs and flowers (optional)

Natural food colouring (optional – you might not want to stain the bath!)

Method

Sift the citric acid and bicarbonate of soda into a bowl. Add the salts, cornflour and decorations, if using. In a separate container, mix the oil, essential oil and natural colouring (if using). Then slowly add the oil to the dry ingredients, until you have the consistency of dampened sand. You may need to wet your hands with the water or add a few drops of it. The mixture needs to hold when you pack it together.

Form small balls and pack them into moulds – or use a fairy-cake/muffin tray. Leave them to set for around 15 minutes (no longer, as they'll stick). No fairy cake/muffin trays? Instead, make bath crumble, by rubbing the ingredients together and sprinkling it into a jar to dry out, and then throw a handful into a warm bath. Easy!

SWEET ROSE SCRUB

Ingredients

To make a jam jar's worth, you will need:

Equal parts of sugar and olive oil (or use coconut
   oil). Measure these, half and half, in the jam
   jar, then scoop the ingredients into a bowl for
   mixing.

Rose oil – a few drops (or you could use lavender
   petals, or any other essential oil)

Dried rose petals (optional)

Method

Mix the sugar with the oil, rose oil and petals, and seal
in a jar. Use a spoonful when you're in the shower as a
body scrub.

Notes: The sugar can be brown or white, and if you
don't have sugar, you could use salt. For the oil, olive is

fine and so is coconut, or go for almond oil. There's no need to splash out on expensive, extra virgin organic olive oil (but that said, you don't want to spread chip fat on yourself either).

LAURIE'S TOP TIPS

If you're eating an avocado, Don't waste the skin! Once you've scooped out the flesh, rub the inside of the avocado skin on your elbows (or knees). Instant moisturizer!

Lots of squashy over-ripe fruit that you think is past the smoothie/milkshake/spread-it-on-toast stage can be great for a face mask. Don't chuck it! Mash it up, and add yogurt or oats, if you like. Mangoes, bananas, strawberries are all ideal.

Or how about a foot mask? Mash a banana with a teaspoon of olive oil, and slather it over your feet. Leave it for ten minutes, before rinsing it off. It's a perfect skin softener. (Do this in the bathroom so you don't stain the sofa!)

Want a quick makeover? Wipe a slice of raw beetroot on your lips to give them a natural glossy colour. Or freeze a blueberry and dot it on to your eyelids for a bit of colour.

 Did you know you can freeze bananas? If you have a recipe that calls for a quarter of a banana, say – and you don't want to eat the rest – stick the leftovers in the freezer. Then eat them as they are (they're delicious dipped in peanut butter), or put them into a food blender, and whizz them into ice cream.

A Note from the Author

Probably the trickiest part of writing this book was doing it with mashed bananas and oats on my face. Still, you've got to live it, right? And while I've not yet found a Toffee Pops skincare miracle (the search goes on, people!) I really do think it's a cool idea to make face masks and lip scrubs from ingredients in the kitchen.

It's not a new idea, of course. Using natural ingredients in cosmetics and skincare goes back thousands of years. The Ancient Egyptians are said to have moisturized their skin with olive oil and sesame oil; the ingredients of face masks in Ancient Rome included rose water, olive oil, and almond oil; and the women of the imperial court in Heian Japan are said to have used Yu-Su-Ru (the water used from rinsing rice) when they were combing their long, beautiful hair.

Fast forward to the Victorian era in Britain and there were lots of DIY beauty recipes around (many with dodgy ingredients that are best skipped) including pouring cold tea over your hair, soaking flowers in water to make facial washes (like a toner) and sweet almond cold creams.

And some of my happiest childhood memories (in the 1970s/80s, not the Victorian era) are of my sisters and me in our garden, shaking jam jars of water and rose petals to make 'perfume' with our Mum. I think that's where the idea for Laurie and Fern's beauty recipes came from.

While I was writing this book, I was also thinking about my journalism work. Over the years, I've spoken to lots of people who are finding new ways to reduce food waste and help us to eat in a way that protects our planet – one that's good for people and animals too.

In fact, the idea for the book partly sprang from a year-long column I wrote for the *Guardian* called 'Goodbye Supermarkets'. During that time, I was inspired by conversations I had with people like River Cottage's Hugh Fearnley-Whittingstall (have you seen the BBC's *War on Plastic with Hugh and Anita?* Laurie and Fern would love the one about reducing the plastic in your bathroom!), eco-chef Tom Hunt (a really awesome award-winning chef and author of *Eating for Pleasure, People & Planet*) and I presented a video for the *Guardian* with a totally brilliant foraging expert Fiona Bird (author of *Let Your Kids Go Wild Outside*, and *Seaweed in the Kitchen*).

As I spoke to these experts and wrote about how to buy/grow/forage food in different ways, I also learnt more about food waste: did you know a third of the food that we produce in Britain never even gets eaten? How can that even be happening, when an estimated 3.7 million children in the UK are unable to afford a healthy and balanced diet?

The food waste we produce at home is only a small part of the problem. But buying and eating thoughtfully means we can minimize our own food waste. There are lots of fantastic organisations that help to reduce food waste too, making sure we can access food when we need to, or giving away any extra that we might have (check out UKHarvest.org. uk, the Olio app, and the Real Junk Food Project, for starters).

Those of us that can, should also work together to put pressure on governments and those in the food industry – particularly supermarkets – to help fix our food system and make it work in a fairer way for everyone.

I think Laurie has the right idea when she says that small actions can change the world. And putting some overripe fruit on your face (so it doesn't end up in the bin), is what I call a #plasticfree everyday action, that can help us make a dent in those food waste statistics. Yes, it's a small thing! But if we all made these climate-friendly changes every day, just imagine what we could achieve.

Have you tried any homemade beauty recipes, do you have a great idea to share about reducing food waste, or want to talk more about Laurie, Fern and their friends? Please drop me a note and say hello . . .

Twitter: @byesupermarkets
www.joanneoconnell.co.uk

Acknowledgements

I am indebted to my fantastic agent Claire Wilson at RCW Literary Agency. Thanks so much for believing in this story, Claire. I'm so lucky to have you! I'm also indebted to my editor Lucy Pearse at Macmillan Children's Books (not only an exceptional editor but she makes the best Lemon Drizzle cake, ever). Claire and Lucy – I owe you both so much! Thanks for making my dream come true.

I want to extend that big thank you to everyone at Macmillan Children's Books – with a special mention to Samantha Smith, Simran Sandhu, Cate Augustin on the editorial team, and typesetter Tracey Ridgewell, publicity manager Sabina Maharjan, and Cheyney Smith in marketing. From editorial to design, sales, publicity, and rights, I really appreciate having the support and enthusiasm of so many super-talented people. I also want to say a huge thank you to illustrator Sara Not, for her bubbly bath time artwork and Rachel Vale for creating such a bright and gorgeous cover.

And I'm hugely grateful to the early readers (shout out to Sarah Stewart) and reviewers of the book (Carlie Sorosiak – a massive thank you!) and to all of the children's booksellers, librarians, teachers and bloggers who champion children's books and help stories find their place in the world.

Big hugs go to my lovely Mum and Dad – with thanks for all you've taught me about standing up for what I believe in – to my ace sisters, Donnamarie and Katrina and awesome nephew George, thanks for all the fun, love and support.

Finally, I want to say a million thanks to my amazing husband John, and our incredible daughters Ella and Clara. There are no words big enough to describe how much I love you. But this book has 50,058 words. And this book is for you.

Turn the page for an exclusive extract of *Binderella*, the next brilliant story from Joanne O'Connell

"No one is without difficulties, whether in high or low life, and every person knows best where their own shoe pinches."

— *Abigail Adams*

CHAPTER ONE

'Stop acting like it's an emergency! It's not the end of the world to wear your school uniform on wear-your-own-clothes day.'

'But it is! A fashion emergency is literally *the worst*!' Cassie smacked the palm of her hand against her forehead. 'If there was one day I should have got things right, it was today. I can't believe this is happening to me!'

'Like you couldn't believe you forgot your PE kit last week or that you hadn't done your History homework?' said her cousin Emelia, who was two years older than Cassie. 'Or that you'd left your coat tied around a tree trunk on the playing field—'

'This is completely different, it really matters!' said Cassie, breathlessly. 'You know my best friend, Azra?

Well she says that the first non-uniform day of our high school career is the biggest of our lives. That it's basically our *fashion debut*.'

Emelia rolled her eyes. 'Azra says a lot of things . . .'

Cassie spun around in her seat to look out of the bus window. It was half-past-eight in the morning and already the bus had reached the pizza place on the outskirts of the village. That meant they had ten minutes, tops, before they pulled up outside Silverdale High School.

'But there's nothing you can do now so just try and—'

'Focus,' said Cassie, loudly. She tried to ignore how fast her heart was beating. 'I've got to focus and think of something fast.'

'I don't really see what—'

'Because there is NO WAY that I am going into school dressed like this.'

Cassie pulled at her school skirt. It's called non-uniform day for a reason, she told herself, furiously. NON-uniform! Her mind raced. What could she do to turn this into something better?

Her brain threw up an image of the first ever school uniform from back in the 1550s. If she put her coat on and wrapped her tie around her waist like a sash, she'd look like a Tudor schoolgirl. Yes, technically she'd still be in uniform. But it was a serious style twist . . .

Emelia was looking worried. 'You need to do that breathe through your nose and out through your mouth thing.'

Cassie covered her face with her hands. 'Today's going to be as bad as—'

A surge of humiliation raced through Cassie's body as she remembered how she'd misread the timetable last week and gone to a swimming lesson when she should have been in Spanish. She'd done half a length of the pool before a girl in another form pointed out that she was in the wrong place. Cassie had jumped out, panic-dressed (she'd just thrown her uniform back on over her swimming costume) and raced, dripping wet, to the classroom. The whole class had exploded with laughter.

Emilia lowered her voice. 'Wet Spanish?'

'In fact, it's worse because—'

'Nothing is worse than wearing a swimming costume in front of—' She gave Cassie a friendly shove. 'Apart from when you wore those flowery knickers as a hat to my birthday party.'

'I was three, Emilia!'

Emilia was delving into her bag for her breakfast. 'OK! No need for a full-on Cassie meltdown. Remember what we said about being calm on the bus?' Emilia unwrapped her poppy seed roll, tore it in two and gave Cassie half. 'A good morning can make a better day . . .'

Cassie's shoulders did an involuntary shiver. 'And now all that money I spent on that grey sweatshirt is wasted—'

Emilia looked surprised. 'Grey sweatshirt? That's a bit this century for you! Weren't you going to wear your 1920s flapper dress?'

Cassie felt a sharp jab of pain, like she'd pricked her finger with a needle. She didn't even want to think about how much she wished she was wearing that dress.

Cassie loved fashion history. Whenever she couldn't sleep at night, she recited the timeline of frocks, from funky bead net dresses (high fashion for the Egyptians), to eighteenth century elaborate hoop skirts, to the dresses over jeans trend in the 2000s (what was everybody thinking?).

She loved wearing clothes from different eras. She had a genuine 1960s mini skirt that used to be her Gran's; a purple square neck top from a charity shop that looked Tudor, and now – the pièce de résistance – a shimmering gold beaded 1920s style dress, which her parents had given her for her twelfth birthday. It had the iconic drop waist, which felt roomy and comfy, a shiny gold ribbon threaded around the neckline and an irresistible swish to the skirt.

At home, Cassie liked to go what she called 'Full Flapper' and dance around the flat with her Mum's scarf tied in her bobbed hair. For non-uniform day, though, she'd planned to wear the dress like a pinafore, with a tee-shirt underneath, and her chunky trainers. Timeless with a twist, it was a perfect example of Cassie's favourite look: 1920s cocktail party meets 2020s style.

But Azra had said NO WAY. According to her, letting people know you were a hundred years behind the fashion curve was one of the biggest mistakes you could make at high school. And besides, Azra wanted them to go matchy-matchy.

Cassie swallowed. 'The thing is, we're having the non-uniform day to help launch the Friendship Festival. And Azra said the best way to celebrate everything our friendship has accomplished was—'

'Accomplished?' Emilia showered her in crumbs. 'You've only known each other three weeks!'

Cassie flinched. Who cared how long it had been? When you knew, you knew. And from the first moment Cassie had walked into 7B's form room and Azra had leapt up yelling 'Hair Twins!' – she and Cassie both had crown braids – she knew they would be Best Friends Forever.

Azra was warm, friendly, and excitable. She had

a thick fringe she could flip up and down like a stage curtain, and a loud, oversized laugh. When Azra found something funny she could bring the whole class to a standstill. Already, Cassie and Azra were super close. They ate their sandwiches together, signed off messages with a string of BFF emojis and whenever the teacher asked them to work in twos, she and Azra would just pair off without speaking.

Cassie bit her lip. 'Azra thought that wearing the same grey sweatshirt would be a visual statement about the closeness of our friendship.'

Emilia couldn't reply because her mouth was full. But she looked like she was trying to arrange her face into a non-judgy expression.

Cassie cringed thinking about the messages from Azra, with links to products and the words: ADD TO CART!!!!!!! It had just been her birthday so there was no way she could ask Mum and Dad to buy her something else. And when she'd suggested buying the sweatshirt and accessories with her own pocket money, her Mum had pointed out that Cassie's allowance had already gone on glitter pens and a pom-pom keyring in the shape of a watermelon (which Azra said was to die for).

Cassie pretended it didn't matter. But for the rest of the day, she saw that sweatshirt everywhere. At breakfast, it was on her social media; in the afternoon, the girl in the queue next to them at the supermarket was wearing it and by teatime, even the clouds in the sky were forming themselves into sweatshirt shapes. Then, just before bed, Cassie's phone buzzed with a promo code, for 25% off the sweatshirt. *Offer ends at midnight* . . . Her Mum's eyes had visibly warmed when she heard about the price drop and she offered Cassie an advance on her October allowance. Seconds later, at the virtual checkout, Cassie screen grabbed the magic words: *your order is complete!* and sent them to Azra, who responded with a chain of dancing BFF emojis.

Now though, Cassie's hand flew to her neck. 'What's she going to say when she sees I'm not even wearing my chain with the dangly pineapple!'

Emilia brushed some poppy seeds off her skirt and started scrolling through her phone. 'My advice is not to waste emotion on a fruit-based accessory.'

Suddenly, the bus jolted forward, and Cassie's head jerked up to the window. They'd reached the crossroads, opposite the pub, which meant that the shiny copper and glass school buildings were about to swing into sight.

Cassie's brain snapped into focus.

She yanked her PE kit on to her lap and pulled out her trainers. She shoved them on. There had to be something else she could wear, there just *had* to be. She tipped her satchel upside down, was there any chance she had a spare T-shirt? Pencils, sandwiches, fruit, biscuits and books fell all over the bus seat.

'What are you doing?' Emilia scrambled around, picking things up.

'Looking for a paper bag to put over my face. I need something to cover me up so that no one—'

As the bus lurched around the corner; Cassie

nearly lost her balance. She grabbed her cousin's arm to steady herself. Emilia's mac was so baggy that she hardly noticed.

Wait!

Cassie stared at her fist full of bright yellow fabric. The Amboise mac – that was the name of Emillia's coat – was so oversized; it was basically a two-person tent. Her heart pounded. *I could wear nothing, or my pyjama top, even a bikini under that mac, and no one would be able to tell. I'll literally be hidden in plain sight.*

No way! This was PERFECT.

She moved faster than she ever had in her entire life. Within seconds, she'd tucked her PE shorts on underneath her skirt, whipped off her skirt, jumper and school tie.

Emelia did a double take. 'What's going on?'

'I need to borrow your coat!'

Emilia looked totally confused. She threw her coat over to Cassie.

'Thank you!' Cassie's fingers desperately ran up and

down the sides of it, trying to find the zips, buttons, or press studs.

The bus was pulling up at the bottom of the school driveway. Emilia was sweeping up the rest of the books and snacks.

Emilia grabbed Cassie's arm, and hauled her down the steps, just in time. As they ran towards the gates, Cassie felt a burst of confidence. She loved everything about the mac with its swingy, ripples of fabric. No wonder everyone on the internet was raving about how *the Amboise* was this year's most affordable way to totally re-boot your outerwear. And the COLOUR! An unbeatable block of red, underscored by sunshine yellow. *And yes, underneath I am wearing my PE kit*, she thought. *But no one will EVER know. This mac is life changing! It practically redefines happy fashion . . .*

Emilia opened the door of the student entrance.

'I want to give you a massive hug, Em, and say a proper thanks! But I can't let go of this until I find the fastenings—'

The door swung back and hit Cassie in the face. By the time she'd rubbed her cheek and rearranged her coat so she had a free hand to push the door open again, Emilia was halfway down the corridor.

Cassie yelled at her. 'How do you do this thing up?'

'You can't!' shouted Emilia, as she disappeared around the corner. 'It's a buttonless mac. It's meant to hang loose!'

Cassie flattened her back against the wall of the corridor. *Who cares if this mac is so new it's straight off the catwalk? This is a TOTAL DISASTER.* She caught sight of her reflection in the glass windows of the corridor. *OMG. I look like a walking shower curtain.*

'Watch it!' said Tyler Thompson, as Cassie nearly smacked right into him.

'Sorry' said Cassie, automatically.

Tyler and his friends Alys and Zeke – or TAZ, as they called themselves – were right behind her.

Cassie shuddered. She couldn't stand TAZ. They

said things like 'life's not perfect but your trainers can be' and if anyone had something new, like a pencil case or a water bottle, Tyler, Alys and Zeke insisted on what they called 'authenticating it', to check if it was from a cool brand. They'd made Keely Johnson cry last week because they called her new daisy-patterned backpack a cheap copy.

Tyler eyed Cassie's coat like a panther does its prey. Zeke and Alys exchanged shocked "what-is-she-wearing looks". Cassie instinctively pulled the sides of her coat together.

There was an awkward pause.

'It's not World Book Day, you know.' Alys ran her fingers through her shiny hair, which was every colour of autumn.

Cassie's chest went tight with panic. Alys had a point. The sheer size and vibrancy of the mac made it costume adjacent. *What was I thinking?*

Tyler and Zeke sniggered.

'I just was on my way to—' Cassie nodded her head

in the direction of the loos.

Tyler tried to contain a laugh. 'Find some honey?'

Zeke clapped his hands over his mouth. Alys looked appalled. 'Tell me that you haven't dressed up as Pooh Bear?'

Cassie's face went hot. 'Of course, I haven't dressed up as—'

'He wears that cropped red jacket and that mac is so big and yellow that—' Tyler broke off, as if he couldn't even finish the sentence it was that hysterical.

Cassie took a deep breath and tried to get past TAZ. But she and Tyler did that annoying thing where they both moved at the same time, and her way was blocked.

'Sorry,' said Cassie again.

Just as she thought they'd let her go; Tyler made an elaborate show of opening the door. Cassie felt herself being shoved into the form room.

'People!' said Tyler, theatrically. 'Let's give a big 7B welcome to a very special visitor from the one-hundred-acre wood . . .'

There was a loud scraping of chair legs on the floor. 'No way!' Azra shrieked. 'You've got an AMBOISE?' She leapt up from her seat. 'Let-me-see, let-me-see!' Azra ran over to Cassie and started stroking her sleeve, like it was a new-born puppy. 'It's a real *Amboise*, isn't it? Wow!'

The three heads of TAZ were bobbing around like meerkats. They shoved past Cassie on the way to their desk. Alys looked thunderous, and Tyler snapped: 'Well you didn't recognize the brand either!'

'You're so full of fashion surprises!' squealed Azra. Her curls, pinned with the sparkly hair slide Cassie was supposed to have bought too, looked phenomenal, and she was grinning so hard she looked like a real-life excited emoji.

'It means we can still do the twinning thing, too,' Azra clapped her hands together. 'Because there's no way you're keeping this to yourself! Let's wear half each!'

What? Cassie's stomach turned.

'I'll put my arm in the left sleeve, and you have yours in the right,' Azra blew her fringe up, as she looked at the mac. 'Then as well as twinning with the grey sweatshirt we could share an outer layer!'

'To show your layers and layers of friendship,' said a girl called Esme, solemnly.

Cassie could feel the room beginning to spin. 'The thing is, it's my cousin's coat. I've got to look after it, and not, you know, stretch it.'

'We need to verify that this coat is a genuine Amboise,' said Zeke, stepping into Cassie's way.

Azra had floated back to their desk, flopped onto the chair and was looking at her phone. Esme and the others were all back to their desks too, avoiding eye contact.

'Going to need that coat,' repeated Zeke.

'Or what?' said a loud, cross voice.

Cassie's head whipped around. Fern Larksie was sitting at the back of the room. Fern was into *trashion*- things like wrap skirts made from old curtains. She was currently twisting a silver juice carton into what looked like a set of hair clips. Emelia was best friends with Fern's sister, Laurie, and Cassie had told her all about how Fern had blazed into 7B's form room on the first day of school, wearing a homemade uniform. She'd delivered a speech about sweatshops, planet-polluting fabric and how she'd stitched together her navy skirt from fabric she'd rescued from landfill.

Alys looked Fern up and down – she was wearing inky-blue dungarees with a pea green top. 'At least you're not dressed in crisp packets today.'

'Label, please,' Zeke said firmly, like he was a teacher confiscating a phone.

'The thing I don't get,' Fern continued. 'Is why your love of an item increases by 100% once you *validate* its authenticity. If you like the coat, you like the coat, so who cares where—'

Alys's natural glow faded. 'It's only a bit of fun!'

Fern shook her head. 'No, it's not.'

Alys pointed at Cassie. 'She doesn't mind.'

Fern stood next to Cassie. 'She looks like she minds.

This is what I call Brand Bullying.'

Alys did an eye roll. 'Brand b-u-l-l-y-i-n-g. Oooh big words.'

Cassie knew exactly what Fern meant. She also knew brand bullying was nothing new. Even the Georgians did it, according to her fashion history book. If someone turned up to a ball in an old, unfashionable dress, the footmen wouldn't even let them through the door.

Fern scowled at him. 'The thing is, Cassie, if people like you, who probably *are* wearing the real thing, can't stand up to brand bullies, then it's much harder for others—'

'Get on with it,' snapped Alys.

Cassie knew she should say something powerful and heartfelt about how Fern was right, and labels didn't matter. But every time she looked at Alys' face the words wouldn't come out.

Just then, the door swung open and Mr Jackson, their form teacher strode in. 'Thought I'd come in casual clothes too,' he announced, as he plonked his bag down.

Everyone's head shot up. Mr Jackson was wearing jeans, a T-shirt which said 'this is what a feminist looks like' and trainers that looked like they'd time travelled from the 1990s.

Alys' mouth dropped open. 'This is what a fashion crime looks like.'

There was a general murmur of agreement.

Mr Jackson clapped his hands. 'Sit down everyone! You can thank me for being the coolest form teacher ever, later,' he smiled, as he started the register.

Five and a half hours, and several dodgy moments later – like when Cassie's hand automatically shot up to answer a question in Maths – it was nearly the end of the day and Cassie had survived, coat in tact. She'd done a good job of pretending not to notice Azra's increasingly desperate attempts to show her the sweatshirt and pretended she needed the loo so often that Azra had asked her if she needed to go to see the school nurse. Now all she had to get through was Assembly.

Ms Millar, the head of Lower School strode on to the stage. The big screen came on, with the words: *The Friendship Festival*.

Ms Millar smiled. 'We know that friendships aren't always how they seem on social media, where people can be effusive and exuberant, and look like they've got a BFF for life. At school, things aren't glittery and full of hearts and . . .'

Azra gave Cassie a nudge. 'Well, it is for us!'

Cassie felt a flush of warmth.

'But the friends you make here are real, with all the ups and downs that come with that. And they can be a wonderful part of your time here at Silverdale High, which is why we're going to work together to organise a Friendship Festival. But we need a little help . . .'

There was an interested murmur.

Miss Millar began to explain about the friendship festival that would take place in three weeks' time. To prepare for it, everyone in Year Seven needed to create a piece of work about friendship. Something they could bring along to display or perform at the festival.

Irina, who was on the other side of Azra, started talking loudly about how she loved doing illustrations so she might do one on friendship; Tarone and Alex Barkly were already designing a tribute to their friendship in Lego; and Alys was telling Tyler and Zeke that she'd message them later with a plan once she'd decided what they'd be doing.

'Let's display our new fruity pendants!' Azra held hers up to the light.

Cassie looked unsure. 'Aren't we meant to create something?' Her immediate idea had been to design their own hats and wear them to the festival.

Ms Millar clapped her hands for silence. 'Now, to help officially launch our Friendship Festival, Olivia and Natori, our helpful sixth formers are looking for volunteers to come up on stage and take a Friendship Pledge that we can all try and live by . . .'

Olivia grabbed the microphone. 'OK! First up, I'm looking for friends to pledge to Always Be Kind to Each

Other.'

A pair of boys in 7A were picked. They grinned and Natori snapped his phone. The image instantly appeared on the big screen. *We pledge to be kind to each other.*

Olivia did her jazz hands. 'Who'd like to take a pledge to respect your friends?'

'Let's do this!' Azra whacked Cassie on the arm. 'Put your hand up! We need to be chosen.'

Cassie's heart was in her mouth. She was so close to the end of the day, there was NO WAY she could wreck things now. She put her hand up halfway, hoping it wouldn't be visible from the stage. For a second, Olivia's eyes rested on her. Cassie pretended to have a coughing fit, so her hand came down. Olivia's gaze moved on. A group from 7D were chosen.

Natori and Olivia carried on, working their way through pledges about having fun together, and telling each other if you have something stuck in your teeth.

Azra was getting increasingly agitated. 'We need to

get in there.'

'Next up,' said Olivia. 'Is a pledge about how friendship is about sharing—'

'We can do that!' yelled Azra. 'We've even got the same sweatshirts on because we share the same taste in fashion! And we're even sharing a coat.' She pointed at Cassie's sleeve. 'If anyone can take this pledge it's us!'

There was a shocked silence.

Olivia laughed. 'Well, we can't fault your enthusiasm! Do you and your friend want to come up?'

Azra was already up and making her way along the row, getting people to stand up as she raced past. Cassie sat rigid in her seat, as she grappled with what was happening.

She pulled herself to her feet and feeling like she was wearing the world's heaviest platform shoes, she made her way up to the stage. All she could feel was every single person in Year Seven staring at her. Every cell in her body was going into panic mode.

'We've got matching tops on!' Azra announced, as

they reached the stage. She flashed her eyes at Cassie. 'Take off your coat.'

'Please don't make me do this.'

Natori came right over. 'I don't like having my photo taken either,' he said, his voice dripping with sympathy. 'Why do you think I'm the one behind the camera?'

Olivia smiled. 'How about you stand in the middle, Cassie, and your friend and I will hold your hands to support you?'

'Thanks, but—'

'Great idea,' Azra snapped.

'Let's count down,' said Olivia, encouragingly. 'One . . . two . . .'

Natori lifted his phone to take the photo. Azra and Olivia leant in to pick up Cassie's hands.

'Three!'

As the camera flashed, Cassie's arms were pulled up high, like she was a puppet. Her coat flew open. And captured forever on the big screen, was the cringe-inducing image of Cassie in her PE kit, Azra's expression of pure shock, and the words: Friendship is about sharing.

About the Author

Joanne O'Connell is a journalist, author and copywriter. When she's not writing (for national newspapers and glossy magazines) Joanne loves whipping up #noplastic homemade beauty recipes, from strawberry bath slushies to minty chocolate lip balm.

She occasionally pops up on television and radio, lives in the countryside, with her husband, daughters, and their dog. You can find her on Twitter @byesupermarkets.